With
Animal

With Animal

Carol Guess and Kelly Magee

Black
Lawrence
Press

Black Lawrence Press

www.blacklawrence.com

Executive Editor: Diane Goettel
Cover and book design: Amy Freels

Published 2015 by Black Lawrence Press.
Printed in the United States.

To

Gus and Audrey Magee-Kenney, Kelly's wild human animals

and

Caroline, Jake, and Kelly Fitton

MR. WISE: *We have so much, Your Honor.*

Steven Wise, Nonhuman Rights Project,
"Transcript of the Hearing re. Tommy," 12/3/13

Contents

With Dragon   1

With Horse   5

With Fish   10

With Sparrow   16

With Human   25

With Sheep   29

With Joey   35

With Unicorn   37

With Jellyfish   45

With Replica   50

With Me   59

With Spider   66

With Stone Lion   71

With Egg   72

With Cat   80

With Snakes   84

With Squirrel   89

With Killer Bees   94

With Storm   103

With Locust   105

With Fox   111
With Plush   118
With Sloth   120
With Raccoon   124
With Hippo   131
With Nebula   140
With Animal   142

With Dragon

The change appeared like the onset of a fever. Her skin ached. Her legs threatened collapse. Though heat welled in her, she shivered and heaped blankets on her body. Her husband stopped sleeping with her, complaining that she steamed up the room. Her side of the bed darkened with stains that looked like scorch marks. Sometimes, when the baby's roiling woke her in the early morning, she watched breath curl from her nostrils in long plumes.

The books said a rise in body temperature was normal. They also said that unnatural cravings should not be indulged.

The XXX salsa was too mild. The mug of boiling water too cool. At the grocery store, she bought tuna steaks and corn syrup. Ate the tuna from the wrapper on the way home. Caramelized the syrup on the stove and swallowed a spoonful straight from the bubbling pan. Removed the pan and looked at the flame circling the burner. Salivated.

It was as she suspected. This baby was after more than just heat.

○

The question was not if, but how. Shotgunning seemed best. There was a fair amount of control one needed to exercise in the throat. Getting it to the stomach was key. Once there, it'd be broken into constituent parts that could be delivered directly to the baby. So said the message boards, other women like her who'd rejected their doctors' instructions. They traded illegal recipes and animated emoticons. They reminded each other to *Fight the good fight!* and *Do it for the kids!* and *Trust your instincts, mama!* They complained about hardheaded husbands and infected interior burns. They shared wisdom from handbooks no longer printed: "Infants in the womb who are denied this crucial element are born with immature fire glands and lack the capacity to ignite." They argued over methods but agreed that non-eaters were handicapping their children. *Why not amputate their wings, too?* she wrote, eliciting a round of virtual applause. No one on that board knew that she had yet to take the first swig.

○

The message boards didn't convey how excruciating an eater's pregnancy could become.

○

Her hair turned brittle. Her tongue swelled. Her eyes blinked back globs of mucous. Blood pulsed heavily through her veins. But consumption only strengthened her craving. Now the women on the message boards warned her: *moderation, mama!* And, *Easy does it. You don't want to create a little monster!*

She wrote, *Do you ever feel like your baby is stronger than you?* To which the message boards replied nothing.

She wrote, *Do you ever wonder if you've made a mistake?* but she didn't bother to check the replies.

○

When the day came, the sky hung wreathed with fire. She stood in the kitchen, smoke peeling from her thighs, fire breaking instead of water, water what might put her out. Her husband splashed orange juice on her skirt. Ran red lights until lights stopped turning. Hustled her into the emergency room with the D word: Dragon.

Because such births were not to be treated casually.

Because such births were not to take place unwitnessed.

○

She'd heard stories on the message boards, which flashed red when someone posted A Disappearance. Usually it was mothers who disappeared, leaving ash and a hungry child. But sometimes fathers got too close, bent to listen where the heart should be.

It was unfortunate about her husband.

Everyone said so.

He'd been such a good man.

○

Raising a baby dragon alone wasn't what she'd imagined for herself. In sixth grade she wanted to be a princess and live in a castle. In seventh grade, a fire fighter. Now she was both, sort of; not really. The baby slept soundly. He was learning to crawl.

○

The message boards kept her company at night. *How do I keep his lunch box from melting?* and *Does anyone use night breathing for cooking?* She ferried words back and forth, Dragon curled in her lap, now pressed to her shoulder. Now sitting beside her in a homemade chair, slit in the back for his long green tail.

For Valentine's each year, red heart on felt: *I love my mother.*

Now standing, now stooping in their low-ceilinged rooms.

◯

The women on the message boards said little when she asked about The Flyaway. *Sad*, someone wrote, followed by frowning emoticons. Someone else posted a link to a video: a winged shape rising, hovering over green trees.

She wrote, *How do I prepare?* To which the message boards replied nothing.

She wrote, *What will I love when he flies away?* but she didn't bother to check the replies.

◯

One morning she woke early and stumbled to the window. Her son stood in sunrise on a skein of scorched lawn. His wings stretched the length of her car, the car she'd promised to give him if only he'd stay. While she watched, he staggered, flapping. Tried to lift off. Hovered briefly, crashed down.

She no longer needed the message boards. She knew without asking that flying meant leaving. Not this morning, not this afternoon, but summer, soon.

She could smell the forest burning.

With Horse

She'd expected that being a single mom of twins would be difficult, but the girls mothered each other. They brayed when separated, slept with limbs entwined just like on the ultrasound. One knobby, one plump. No one thought they were related. People thought pet, not sibling. Owner, not twin. But the girls paid attention to no one. They'd swum together as embryos before anyone had known they existed. She'd known the medicine increased the risk of multiples, but even so, hers was a rare kind of pregnancy. High risk, both before and after the girls were born. Risk of discordant fetal growth. Of heart conditions. Of colic and tetanus. Later, of bonding problems. Of favoritism.

She didn't have a favorite. But the girls preferred each other.

They took bottles from her and fed themselves. They spent so much time lying on the floor nose-to-nose, giggling, that their hair—the same chestnut color—tangled them together. They screamed when she tried to comb out the knots, so now they had identical missing patches where she'd cut them out instead. The human galloped around the yard; the horse sat at the breakfast table. Their sharing left room for the limitations of the other. The horse rarely went full speed; the human wouldn't use her digits.

They were going to be developmentally delayed. That much was clear.

They were never going to marry.

In her dreams, the girls rode each other in the sunset.

Equine temper tantrums were worse than human ones. But only humans could say, *We wish you weren't our mother.*

She called the girls bilingual, but the reality was that the human spoke for the horse. *She's scared of that van*, the girl said when the horse bucked on an afternoon walk. Or, *She thinks she's in danger.* Or, *She's worried you're going to send her away.*

Or, when the mother showed them her worn copy of *Black Beauty*, *She hates that book.*

What's wrong with it?

The girl answered, *The horses are dumb. And the people are mean.*

The horse snorted over her shoulder, big, yeasty breaths. Too big for the couch now, so she stood behind it. The mother remembered their birth, the fast labor, the buzzing of the NICU team—the foal severely premature, the infant severely overdue. Few of these pregnancies went to term, and of those that did, fewer resulted in two live births. The OB-DVM had recommended termination: her choice, which fetus. They'd made her sign waivers. Convinced her to deliver in front of a roomful of witnesses. *Most of them*, the OB-DVM told her, *will never see a birth like this again.*

Now her twins leaned against each other, identical looks of disgust at the book in their mother's hands. She eyed them carefully. Already it was hard to imagine what they were thinking. She missed them as babies, when they'd needed her for small things: to pour the milk and turn on the TV. She couldn't tell how much they understood about who they were. Or what would happen to them.

People can be cruel, she said.

Her daughter flared her nostrils. Tossed her head. *Yes*, she said. *But horses aren't dumb.*

School was out of the question. Instead she gathered books on homeschooling, read the message boards, met with a group once a month. At first she divided the girls' lessons, horse child running agility trials while girl child memorized history. When the twins rebelled, kicking and scattering hay, she concocted lessons that occupied both. The girl studied equine art, history, and literature; the horse set her paces to music and math. Together they learned botanical terms on rides through the woods in the hills above town.

She tracked down the phone numbers of a few other parents raising hybrid twins. The first lived in Iceland and hinted at witchcraft. The second rebuked her for questioning God. The third, a couple, had adopted their children: also both girls, also horse-human. She was so excited by their story, similar down to the smallest detail. A few weeks later, watching the news, she learned that theirs was a well-crafted hoax. They'd invented horse child, girl child, twin speak, based on the family they wanted to be. They were hybrid fetishists, and they were obsessed. The family they watched and wanted was hers.

○

The neighbors complained about manure in the yard, hoof prints on manicured lawns. They pointed to a city ordinance that forbade farm animals.

She's not a farm animal. She's my daughter.

The neighbors snorted, stamped heels in the dirt.

○

Sometimes the girls fought, turning on each other with the same intensity they gave to love. Usually one of them skulked in the stable while the other wept and nuzzled mother.

It shamed her that she loved this singular closeness almost enough to encourage their fights.

She didn't have a favorite. True, she liked whinnies better than laughs, and reading better than riding. But it would take another child for her to feel favored or play favorites.

She decided to ask the girls how they felt. They carried a picnic lunch to the playground and tossed used horseshoes. After apples, carrots, and sugar cubes she faced them.

How would you like a brother or sister?

Horse neighed and snickered, then galloped in circles around the field.

Human or horse? Girl asked.

It doesn't matter.

It matters to me.

Fine, then. Human.

Girl looked pleased. *Don't tell her, Mom.*

The word *Mom* like stained glass lighting windows of sky.

That was how it started. She'd discovered the winning ticket, word that would bend one child close, closer to her than to her sister. The word was *human* or the word was *horse*. All through her pregnancy she confided in each, whispering to girl that she wanted an infant; whispering to horse that she wanted a foal.

Surely when the baby arrived they would forget keeping secrets and stop telling lies.

This pregnancy clicked. This birth was off-camera. A midwife at home, a birth pool of warm water. She sent the girls to stay with a neighbor. The midwife lit candles to welcome her son.

All night she held him, sleeping and nursing. She named him alone and sang their first songs.

The next day, or day after, or the following week, she knocked on the neighbor's door, calling her girls to welcome their brother.

The neighbor handed her a note.

We're safe, it read, *but don't come looking.*

Two by two. She understood.

With Fish

My girlfriend on the sofa, swaddled in blankets. Flossing her teeth while she watches TV.

My girlfriend, drinking coffee and buttering toast, scanning a list of sperm donors, selecting for tall.

My girlfriend, moaning, bent over the bed, my fist inside her where a baby should be.

O

We went to the mall and she wanted a baby. It killed me that I couldn't give her fragments of my DNA; that sex between us was always just sex.

No. It didn't kill me at all. I thought it was funny, ordering sperm in the mail. But queers are supposed to feel apologetic about these things, to make up for the fact that sex is pure pleasure.

She had to order our future baby's father's genetic material through a doctor. She couldn't just have it sent to our house. Of course, she could've walked into a bar, hit on some guy, and conceived our child in an alley. But no, a doctor had to be involved. They made her get tested for HIV, too.

The waiting room was filled with Christian magazines, embroidered pillows, and gendered toys. "You're my sister," she whispered when they called her name, and our relationship slipped behind one of the pillows. Later, she told me that the ceiling was decorated with a mobile of animals, and that the doctor called house pets "little buddies."

"We're going to get you a little buddy of your own," he said, slipping sperm inside her while her sockless feet galloped in stirrups.

"Why didn't you wear socks?" I asked. I always wore socks to the GYN.

"Were you listening at all? He called my baby 'little buddy,' like he knows it's going to be a boy."

"You just called it 'my baby.'"

"This was my idea."

I'm not your sister, I thought. But it was true; the baby was her idea. I'd never wanted to carry a child, by which I meant inside me or even in arms. Children scared me, with their big bug eyes. Besides, why assume you'd get the kind you wanted? Serial killers had to come from somewhere. What if the child was violent or wouldn't stop spinning? Worse, what if it was boring, lived an ordinary life?

We were eating dinner when the doctor called. She was three months in, swimming in dizziness.

"Hello," and pause. "I see. With what?"

She hung up the phone and went straight to the bathroom.

I could hear the tub, smell lavender bath salts.

That night she spit bubbles while she flicked her feet.

O

It took three days for her to tell me about the phone call: her doctor, calling to confess a mistake. He'd inseminated her with the wrong injection. Wrong needle, wrong species. She was pregnant with fish.

"Oh," I said; what was the right thing? "You're beautiful, sweetheart. I've always loved guppies."

She started to cry. "Have you looked at my stomach?" She lifted her blouse, blue billowy cotton. A little bump that glowed and pulsed.

That night and the next I lay awake while she slept, watching her stomach as she tossed in dreams. In the dark of our bedroom her belly lit up, transparent. I could see tiny shapes moving in circles. An aquarium where her roundness should be. Even a castle, green seagrass like glass. A faint sound of gurgling.

At least we knew this of fish: they only grow to the size of their container. But how many was another story. Could be a few catfish, slow and cumbersome. Or dozens of flashing cichlids, forever tiny.

I watched her stomach closely. I counted the shadows she made on the ceiling, tried to pick out tail from fin, until the growing hum of her motor put me to sleep.

O

We weren't telling yet—how did we tell such a thing?—so her coworkers threw us a shower, besieged us with gender-neutral onesies and receiving blankets, t-shirts that said Hatched By Two

Chicks and Love Makes a Family, gift certificates for cleaning services. Her friends had gone back to cloth diapers and homemade baby food, had become punk rock versions of their grandmothers. They carried their babies in complicated wraps and nursed them until they turned five. Their children had shaggy hair and ran naked past the age when it was cute. Their children had elevated vocabularies and no social boundaries. Their children put their unwashed heads in my lap and I had to restrain myself from shoving them off. I looked at my girlfriend and loved her more than ever.

But after the shower, she wondered aloud if she should get rid of the fish, if getting rid of them was even possible.

"No, please," I said, suddenly desperate. "What seems worst?"

She held out her hands, palms up. "I'll never get to hold them."

We returned the shower gifts and went back to the doctor, stared at the tank in the waiting room, dull goldfish with bulging eyes. When the nurse called my girlfriend's name, I stood in the corner refusing to look at the birth announcements that lined the wall. My girlfriend stepped onto the scale, held her arm out for the blood pressure gage. I didn't need to lie about being a sister because nobody asked who I was.

The doctor was ready with a check. "Buy a nice aquarium on us," he said, looking at the ceiling. "How's your appetite?"

"Terrible," she said. "I could eat nothing but salt."

He frowned. "Must be a marine species. They're harder."

"Harder how?" I stood so he'd have to look at me, but he still addressed his answer to the ceiling.

"More maintenance. Higher mortality rates."

"Look." I waved a hand in front of his face. "She wants to hold them."

"May I suggest," the doctor said, looking at her, "that you learn how to dive."

My girlfriend in a wetsuit, hanging off a speedboat ladder.

My girlfriend showing me her photos of a wolf eel, an octopus, a nudibranch. Leaning over my computer keyboard, her hair damp and fishy.

My girlfriend in the bathtub, pulling my hand between her legs. When she came, the school inside her swirled into a glittering bait ball. Her stomach puffed out, distended. "I'll be damned," she whispered, panting. "I finally look pregnant."

Water reflected silver off her face. Her breathing slowed, and the bait ball unwound. "We will love them," she said fiercely.

"Sure," I said. "Don't we already?"

She looked worried, but I'd spent the last weekend in the back of the pet store, comparing filtration systems and buying bulk substrate.

I already loved them as much as her. Maybe more.

The aquarium took up half the room. Big enough to climb inside, which she did the first night, naked except for her mask and tank. Silhouettes crowded at the edge of her stomach, like koi in a pond. I got into the tank with her, held my breath and put my ear against her navel. Could almost feel the tickle of their mouths, feeding.

She pushed me away and motioned for me to get out.

Towards the end, she slept in the tank, her belly glowing like a nightlight. I missed her, so I moved my bed beside the place she floated, and sometimes she moved her hair aside to smile at me, and sometimes she did these sexy dances while I masturbated in bed. The fish were born so quietly neither of us noticed. I woke to find my girlfriend missing and the room dark. I turned on a light and saw the school moving around her as a single entity.

She didn't wake. The fish startled at the light and rushed back inside her. And like that, they were unborn again.

The change in her spread. I knew that in late pregnancy the growing fetus could shift things around, shove aside the stomach, pressure the bladder and lungs. Her fish babies didn't grow. Instead, more of her insides flashed on, transparent. I could see her organs now, one the shape of a treasure chest, one a skull and crossbones. Her chest glassed over, and there was her heart, bubbling.

I convinced the doctor to make a house call. She was no longer surfacing to eat.

By the time he arrived, I could see all the way through her. He handed me a check and refused to come upstairs.

In the tank, seaweed blew like hair. The fish followed each other's slightest movements, tracking shapes that looked like a body.

With Sparrow

The bird in my chest may or may not be mine. Something feral led her to me. A bit of uncooked egg, perhaps, and now my body's never still. Sometimes I think of her as trapped. Sometimes I think she's the twin God intended, the excess my body sloughed off to make me.

Friends think I'm joking when I say I'm pregnant. My husband's amused by my appetite: pecans and suet; apples and corn. I shake my head *No* to whiskey and wine. Once a bottle came at me, insistent. I moved my glass as the host started to pour, a splash of red across my skirt.

My husband likes to be inside me every night. He had the surgery years ago, before he met me, when he was running wild. "You're all I need," he says, as his body unclenches. "If I still had bullets, you'd be feeding an army."

My sparrow's wings brush my belly, a message meant for sky, not me.

O

Wednesdays I go out to lunch with the girls from Escrow. So it's Wednesday, so we're eating spaghetti, so I feel something wet run down my thighs. In the bathroom I peel off my hose. Not water, yolk. My sparrow's ready. I squat and push. The scratching knocks me to the floor, but it's so fast, and then she's gone.

I tidy up in the sink, stuff my hose in my purse, and open the door, freeing my bird.

She flies into the restaurant. Diners duck, cover their heads. Someone shouts "Bat!" and grabs a broom. I hold out my arm; when she's circled several times, she swoops, alighting.

I walk out of the restaurant, arm outstretched, chirping. All the way home I worry she'll leave me for finches in gardens or crows on the street. When I reach for my keys she startles, flies into a tree. I hold out my arm and stand very still until she settles. We walk inside, through the kitchen onto the back porch, and I show her the cage.

"This is where I first imagined you," I tell her. The cage is twice the size of my bedroom. I've been preparing for months. Every window has a stained glass bird embedded in glass, so she'll never mistake window for cloud. Perches hang from the ceiling; the floor's littered with twigs, straw, cotton. Two Japanese maples sit in giant pots. There's a birdbath with running water and piles of dirt, complete with worms.

She chirps, so I know she's happy she's chosen me. I sit with her for a while, on a bench in the corner, the only human furniture. Once she's perched on a tree branch I tiptoe out and lock the cage.

There are ways my husband doesn't know me.
Maybe I'll keep this bird to myself.

"Baby, sit on my lap."

I rub my cheek against my husband's chest. I smell beer on his breath and remember the night we met, how I knew right away that he was my destiny. But I never wanted a baby and neither did he. Some people dress up their dogs, call them pet names. Some people make sex into a pet, keep it tethered. I just wanted something moving inside me that wasn't a man or a machine.

I name her Sparrow for the winged sound of the word.

I lose the baby weight. My friends ask me what diet I'm on. "The bird diet," I tell them, and they nod like they know me. But they'll never know me.

She learns to fly in circles to avoid striking glass.

My husband thinks her cage is my workroom, tools for crafts: fabric, yarn, clay. I lock myself inside for hours. He knows not to knock, not to disturb. I've taught him to crow when he needs me. Then I go out, and let him come inside me because he is unfeathered and upright, and it seems that there is still something I crave in the human form.

Sometimes Sparrow flies all night, and I wonder where she would go if windows were clouds.

On Wednesdays, the girls from Escrow complain about sex with their husbands. They buy expensive wine and sex toys, but nothing helps. When it's my turn, I lie and say twice a week. They are impressed; they don't know how I put up with it. They sigh and wish for their twenty-year-old sex drives. They talk about children, and trying for children: sex here for a boy, there for a girl. Someone is charting the moon. Someone is getting her numerology done. Someone is drinking pregnancy tea and buying extra lube. The others nod. All their husbands could try harder. They could all put more effort into foreplay. The girls say they bet my husband is a wild one, an all-night kind of guy. They say I should tell them my secret.

I tell them they should get new husbands.

They laugh, but I'm not joking. It's not polite to tell them that they are responsible for their own unhappiness, but I've been spending so much time alone that I'm saying things I normally don't. I tell them their husbands are losers and I don't know how they put up with it. One of them touches my arm and asks what's wrong, so I tell them I lost a baby. They go misty-eyed, and say all the right things, which are all the wrong things since I didn't really lose a baby. Only later does one of them say she thought my husband got snipped. When I don't respond, there is another round of knowing looks: *affair.* They think they know my secret now, and they disregard everything I've said.

⬤

I stop by the Seed 'N' Feed on my way home. A bag of black sunflower seeds, a stack of suet cakes, and then, on impulse, into a room called the Bird House. The birds all know me, but today something's different. Yellow canaries and finches stare silently at a cage in the corner. A single, dark bird inside. It looks vaguely like Sparrow, a cousin. I chirp to the birds I know but they don't cock their heads. It's the new bird that answers.

"You're sweet," it says. "You're beautiful."

I go to the front desk and ask about the talking bird, am handed a fact sheet for the myna. There is a price at the bottom.

I pay cash.

O

I release Myna into the cage, where he hops around, refusing to fly. My Sparrow is hiding in one of the potted trees. I can feel her eyes on me. Myna whistles and kicks up straw. He looks at the birdbath and says, "This is pretty nice."

I startle. "What?"

"I mean," he says, "way better than my last place."

I try to compose my next thought. All I end up saying is, "You talk really well. Do you think you could teach my Sparrow how to talk like that?"

"Sparrow?" he says. "Aren't they aggressive?"

"She's tame," I say. "I think."

"I could try." Myna hops to the tree she's in, but he doesn't look up. "You know what you ought to get? You ought to get some mosquitoes."

Then, maybe because I just need to talk, I find myself telling Myna the story of Sparrow's birth. I gush about it. I haven't told anyone. He stays under the tree while he listens. At the end of it, I'm embarrassed, apologetic. Sparrow is there, somewhere in the tree, listening. "I don't know why I'm telling you all this," I say.

"It's your incredible story." He shrugs his wings. "People always want to tell me their incredible stories."

"Probably because you're an unusual bird," I say.

"Nah." He pecks at the soil, finds a worm, spits it out. "Talking birds are common. But I've never heard of a lady dropping an egg."

O

On Wednesday, I ask the girls if they've ever heard of a bird that can talk, really talk, make up its own sentences and everything. One tells me about her cousin, who could carry on a whole conversation with her macaw. Another says she saw a video of a bird giving commands to the family dog. They all agree that birds have complex language skills. Then they ask about my husband and call us lovebirds. I don't tell them how my husband and I fucked right before I walked out the door to meet them. I don't tell them what I suspect, which is that a successful sex life means you don't have to talk about it all the time. I don't tell them that my husband and I are good together in one very specific way, but when we've tried to be together in other ways, we have failed.

I say I've been having a dry spell, and the girls smile knowingly.

O

For three days, Myna meets me at the door and tells me not to come in. Things are happening, he says. They are working on a surprise.

For three days, I don't sleep with my husband. He comes home smelling of alcohol, then goes into our bedroom and shuts the door. When I touch him, he pretends to be asleep.

I scatter seed on the lawn, turn on the hose and let the water drain down the drive.

○

The next time I go in, there are no birds to greet me. I step gingerly onto the straw. I haven't cleaned in days, so the room smells musty, birdy. I chirp to let them know I'm there, and in a moment, Sparrow flies down from the window ledge. I see Myna sitting up there still.

Sparrow lands at my feet. In a mechanical-sounding reproduction of Myna's voice, low in her voicebox, she speaks. "Hello. Mama."

The words are garbled and automatic, but I thrill to the sound. "Hello, baby."

"Mama." She sounds determined, but I can't make out the words that follow.

"You're speaking," I say. "It's wonderful." I'm so proud of her, so drunk on her voice, that I'm unprepared for what she does next. She attacks. She flies at me feet-first, and before I can think about it, I've reacted. It's over fast. I scream something very birdlike, and there's a clash, and then Sparrow is on the ground. "Crazy bird," I say, shaking. "Crazy bird."

She gets up and limps off. Myna says nothing as I leave. I want to go to my husband, but he's not there, so I take a sleeping bag, spread it outside the door to the cage. For hours I listen to their murmuring through the wall.

○

My husband comes home, and I demand to know who he's been with. He tells me. It doesn't change anything. We fuck passionately, and it is just as good as it was before.

I tell him I want to get a pet. A bird or something. Maybe two birds.

He says birds creep him out. Those beady eyes, he says. And did you know they're related to dinosaurs?

I tell him I won't get one of those. I'll get something sweet, a songbird.

But he says songbirds are just as bad. He wants to know why we need a pet. He thinks we are too busy to take care of it. Me, in my craft room all the time.

"I'm lonely," I say. "That's why."

He tells me a bird would be fine. Two birds, he says. We stay up not talking for a long time.

○

Now on Wednesday, when I complain it's not a lie. I say I haven't slept with my husband in a week, and the girls roll their eyes. *Another dry spell?* I'm a wreck. I can't tell them that I miss my husband, that I've had a fight with my child. I can't tell them that I don't know who belongs to me, and who doesn't, and whether or not anyone ever knows this, or if, instead, we are all just playing at love so we don't have to be alone.

○

I get another bird, a finch that flies around for three days and drops dead. I release butterflies into the cage, and the birds feast on them. "Sparrow," I call, but she is no longer mine. There are so many ways I don't know her. Eventually, I spot a nest in one of the potted trees. Three eggs. My grandbirds.

I baby her, my Sparrow. Bring her twigs from apple trees and new hay for the nest, release mosquitoes and fireflies for dinner. Sparrow and Myna whisper together, but neither speak to me. I do my work silently and leave. I go to my husband. "Baby, come inside me," I say, and he does, and we sleep. We dream that we are all we need.

○

Sparrow meets me at the door. It's been weeks since she's come down while I'm there, maybe longer. "Hello, baby," I say.

"Mama," she says in that same mechanical voice, a voice that bubbles around her voicebox. "Leave."

I look past her, afraid enough not to brush her aside. I know the eggs are hatching. I know they've hatched. I want to see the babies. I want to see if they're anything like her, or me, or my husband, or Myna. I want to know what's real and what's not.

"Myna," I shout. "Tell me what's happening."

"There's something wrong with the babies," he says from the nest.

"Mama. Leave," Sparrow says.

I brush past her, and she lets me go. The nest smells like her. Inside, there are three cracked eggs. Three splatters of color, red, wrong for a bird.

Three flowers, pistons tipped yellow. Petals like skin.

"They're beautiful," I say to my birds, and they understand what I mean.

The tragedy is in the impossibility. The tragedy is how I could never tell anyone what really happened.

I put the flowers in water. I set them next to the stained glass. I tell the girls from Escrow that my husband bought me a bouquet. I say things are hard, but that we're working it out, like couples do, exactly like couples everywhere are doing, exactly like we're supposed to.

With Human

I.

When she learned that the baby was human, she felt disappointed. It rattled inside her, fearless and furless, alphabet of bones and thumbs.

An animal pregnancy was all soft tongues, lapping; pink silk and decoration. Multiples, so they took care of themselves. They nested inside each other, fully formed at birth.

It wasn't her fault, her husband reminded her. His DNA decided things. He was the carrier; he was the male. Still, she talked to the baby animals. Named them as if she might keep them.

Of course mothers could only keep human infants. Baby animals were whisked away. Her first three pregnancies were bundled in yellow blankets and disappeared down the hall with the nurse. Of course they reassured her that her kittens, puppies, and pandas were loved; cuddled and coddled. Of course she didn't look at the smoke that flew over the hospital, crooked gray birds.

This time it was human, so she could keep it. Her husband would name it, reward her with gifts. She would be given a pink or blue blanket, press a heart to her chest, nurse a face when it cried.

Where were her animals? Where had they gone?

The little human baby snowballed inside her, colder and harder, collecting sharp stones.

2.

Ivy covered the windows of the animal nursery.

Night nurse, fox nurse, noon nurse, God.

3.

Down the hall, human babies failed the APGAR. Neonatal German Shepherds twitched in sleep, hightailing sheep.

4.

She winced when her husband stroked her stomach: Henry, Catherine, Leroy, Lee.

Sit and *Stay*.

He fed her cravings: dog food, cat food, worms, bamboo.

5.

When the baby was born, she felt pleased. He dropped from her like an anvil, dense and singular. Dark hair curled down his back. He didn't suck at her breast so much as gnaw.

He lifted his head right away, arching away from her. She stroked his naked cheek until he turned and bit her finger.

Her husband couldn't swaddle him tight enough. The baby's legs kicked free, bicycling air. Gymnast, her husband said. Escape artist. Strong man.

Animal, she thought. Beloved.

6.

She taught the baby to roll over. To speak for his food. By twelve months he'd learned to wait at his bowl in the morning. By eighteen, he could climb the refrigerator. Evenings, she stroked him in her lap, his limbs tucked under, his soft snores vibrating her belly.

Of course she worried when, by twenty-four months, the sounds he made for food hadn't turned into words—the yips and snaps failed *mamas* and *papas*. Of course she listened when they told her to read to him, sing to him. Once upon a time, she said. ABC, she said. He bared his teeth.

No, she said. Down.

7.

Her husband was served the notice at work. An error, it said; a birth record filed wrong. Wrong name. Wrong species. In bold, a date and address for returning the baby.

We could petition, she said.

Her husband wept. No use, he said.

Their child eyed them, cobbling understanding from pitch and gesture. His mouth groped, tongue pushing teeth, teeth pushing lips. *Maaa*, he said. His intelligent eyes fixed on her.

We'll go, then, she said. Tonight, we'll go.

8.

A gritty haze covered the city. She ran the wipers, and her child quivered, strapped into the back seat. His nose pressed to the window. To the raccoons and turkey vultures scavenging the ditches. At the rest stop, he took off. Bolted straight for the highway. She braced herself, but instead of collision, a flock of birds lifted, broken, into the sky. Her boy beneath them, leaping and gnashing. She called him, and he came loping back.

Good boy, she said. She took him into her arms: her child, her son. From deep in her throat came a guttural sound.

She licked back the hair from his forehead. Nipped at his face. Nosed him back into the car.

Without her husband, there would be no more babies. No more names. No need for her language at all.

With Sheep

I.

Drive, she said, so I did, and then I said, Where to? and she said, I don't know, south? so I veered onto the interstate and gunned it for Lord knows where, weaving through traffic like I knew where I was going, her beside me with feet on the dash, knees open, pants soaked. Do you got the book? she said, and I said, I got the book, and then I glanced into the back seat to make sure I had the book, and it was right there like it'd been the whole last month, this kind of thing not known for its predictability, due dates ranging over several weeks, symptoms unclear—she'd been shedding a lot, could that be a sign?—the best advice the doctor could, *would*, give being, You'll know it when it happens. How will we know? we wanted to know, but her doctor was a prick who thought all woolies should be quarantined or banished, and once he got the tests back he asked us to seek help elsewhere knowing there was

no help elsewhere, knowing there was no elsewhere. Once her coat
came in, she couldn't even ride the bus without getting dirty looks.
Even her parents disowned her, the hypocrites. I told them right to
their faces. What's that you're wearing, I said, and is it or is it not
made from animals?

Her dad had on a wool sweater. I could tell. He said, Not
those kind of animals.

That's what you think, I said.

Her mom said, You two are determined. I can see that. Where
will you do it?

Here was where my girl finally chimed in. In a field, she said
quietly, like she was in a trance. In the moonlight. Under a spring
shower.

She's lost her mind, her dad said.

Had to admit, I thought so, too.

We weren't so much determined as desperate. Her parents
could've given us the money we needed, but when she asked, her
dad gave her a book about financial planning instead. It was called
The Richest Man in Babylon: The Success Secrets of the Ancients. The
first piece of advice was "start thy purse to fattening." So that was
what we did.

Now here we were, driving south to nowhere special, towards
the big unknown, and I was terrified that the big unknown would
come shooting out of her the wrong way, backwards or upside down,
maybe drenched in blood, maybe strangled by its own cord, and I'd
be the only one on deck, standing there with my thumb on chapter
nine. I hadn't studied enough. I sucked at exams. The test material
was all half-wrong anyway, designed for vets and pawned off on
woolies like they didn't still have human anatomy. The factory people

had assured us that she'd go back to being a normal girl within a few weeks of delivery. The injections, they said, are simply for the health of the fetus. The meds may cause some *completely reversible* changes in your girlfriend here, but hey, they said, it'll make her hair nice and thick! Then they'd nudged me and said, Some of the side effects you might enjoy! I still didn't know what they'd meant by that.

Pull over here, now, she said suddenly, so I did because she was panting and grinding her teeth, and because I didn't know where I was going anyway, although she could've picked a friendlier spot, this one being the side of the road and all, and beyond that miles and miles of snow-covered nothing. I grabbed the book and got out, and she twisted free of her clothes and fell onto the gravel, chest heaving. I'd be lying if I said she looked even partly human then. But she wasn't animal either. Three months ago, she'd started covering her body like other woolies, even around me, so it'd been a while since I'd seen her bare skin, but when I rounded the front of the car I could see that she didn't have bare skin anymore, she had this white fur, thick but short, darker in the places she sweat.

I couldn't help it. I bent down and petted her.

The fur looked so soft and my god, it felt even softer, like mink, I thought, though I'd never touched mink, and I confess, yes, my first thought was that if this baby was anything like its mother then were going to get a lot for the trade. We were going to be set for some time.

She'd been lying on her side, groaning, but she shot up after I petted her, got on all fours and tried to kick me with her hind leg. I yelped. She panted and put her head down. I could see that a single leg was hanging out of her. There was no head. That wasn't good.

I'm dying, she said. Help me.

Remember, I said, it's completely natural. This was what she'd told me to tell her, but she didn't seem to want to hear it now. Her eyes glassed over, her face retreated into itself, and she screamed.

I'm a beast! she said. It hurts!

Just calm down, I said. That wasn't the right thing to say either.

She tried to kick me one more time, then her leg twitched around like a dog with an itch, and she ran away across the snowy field. Ran is the wrong word. She was still on all fours. I guess what she did was she galloped.

Where are you going? I shouted. I opened the book in my hands. I looked up *malpresentation of the fetus*. I scanned the words, barely able to make sense of them. *You will need to push the fetus back into the uterus*, I read. *You can use the eye sockets to pull out the head.*

I looked up. She'd stopped galloping and now lay in a heap in the snow.

2.

You looked up. I'd stopped running and now lay in a heap in the snow.

You were waiting for me to birth what would market.

You were waiting for money to fall from my purse.

Here's the secret I'd been keeping under all my fine white fur: no way in hell was I selling my baby. My baby it was, not ours, not yours. My baby's leg, dangling. My baby, struggling to meet me in cold night air. *Woolie*, you called me, like I was a rug. Not human, not animal. Just rolled up to trade.

The car panted on frozen gravel. You stepped toward me, then stopped. Put your head in your book. *Calm down*, paging through chapters. *You can use the eye sockets to pull out the head.*

It was enough that you wanted to sell my baby, but I'd seen the way you looked at my fur. It was common in humans; all woolies said so. You'd put a price on my baby and a price on me, too.

I inched backward, then took off running. Keys in the car, car in drive, driver driving. With a frozen heart still I knew what to do. South, toward snow and something else. If I could get there before the birth. If I could get there at all.

From a distance I watched myself drive, fur fumbling the quicksilver wheel. I watched myself swerve, blood on my thighs, and I watched myself suck on my pain like a lozenge. The barn appeared so quickly that I drove past it, then spun a U-turn on the interstate. Over the median, across winter fields until the car said stop and crashed into a tree.

I don't remember leaving the car or stumbling across the field to the barn. But I remember the door, marked just as she'd promised. No key but a password. The password was *lamb*.

When we stopped being the same (that is, while you stayed stuck in your human ways and I fell in love with my animal instincts), we stopped believing the same stories. You took your news straight, headlined and viral. I bent my ear to what bleated or snaked. There's an underground to every location and at least two versions of every escape.

When I woke up I was surrounded by sheep and my baby was missing. The sheep were circling something. Licking it clean. Black fur wet from blood and tongue. I bent toward her, put my mouth on her, and cleaned my blood from my baby's eyes.

You said I'd change back, that my wool would recede and my skin show taut. You said my humanness would erase all traces of a woolly birth. You said these things because you wanted my baby whether or not I survived the birth. But what had changed in me had made me whole. Now I was who I'd always been. I curled up with my lamb. We slept with our flock.

In the morning, I watched through the diminishing veil of language as my farmer-protector (body like love was once your body) opened the giant door and herded my flock, my family, into a pen.

This was not a slaughter, but a shearing. She'd promised me sanctuary: we could live till we died.

It took a while for her to notice the two of us. I wasn't on my feet just yet, afraid to leave my baby's side.

When she noticed, she smiled. Said something in the language I used to know; it was leaving me, language.

She stroked our wool.

With Joey

When my husband lost the baby, no one understood our grief. We were in clinical trials, the first human subject study approved by the FDA. *At least he's healthy*, my friends said, meaning *At least he didn't die*. What they thought but didn't say was *Why would he do this when you could carry his child?*

The pilot experiments had gone well, but only tested the efficacy of the artificial womb to sustain life, not generate it. Male subjects wore tethered balloons on their stomachs. The early experiments used seeds in soil: roses, violets, and poppies. They bloomed, bouquets. Photos went viral: male models whose rock-hard chests blossomed with flowers.

My husband was not a model. His abs were soft from beer and pie. I was allergic to roses and we both took bad photos. We just wanted a baby. His baby. Not mine.

I never wanted to carry a child. He loved this in me, as he loved all my ways. We planned to adopt, but then he learned from a colleague about the new technology. They were looking for subjects. It was something he wanted, so of course I said yes.

Three days after he lost the baby we were slumped on the couch, watching TV. He'd gone to the hospital that afternoon to have his womb taken off. He was glassy-eyed, weeping at diaper commercials. He scratched his leg, then swatted his knee.

Something just bit me. Does Theo have fleas?

On TV, a tall woman got into a hot tub with her maybe-future-husband.

She's never going to pick him, I said. *It's never the dentist. Always some guy in sales.*

More swatting. Then he jumped off the couch and unzipped his pants. *Something's caught in my pant leg. It feels like a mouse.* He hopped around the living room in boxers, shaking his khakis until his wallet fell out. Nickels and dimes spun to the floor. A small furry something scurried away.

We stared at the tiny creature. It hopped around wildly until it found my husband's leg. Then it dug in and climbed onto his lap. He hadn't lost the baby. The baby had lost him.

I think it's a baby kangaroo.

It probably wants to be swaddled. Will you get me a towel?

I picked out the softest towel I could find. My husband stroked its fur, then wrapped it loosely with its head peeking out.

We named him Joey, because he was. Like all joeys he'd fallen and scrabbled back up. Now he wanted a bottle. To be cuddled and swaddled while watching the world from a makeshift pouch.

With Unicorn

Let's just say I was in high demand. All of the personal ads confirmed it: the inevitable man-woman couple looking for a female third. This third was supposed to be blonde and big-breasted, show up giggling, and promptly undress. I had my pick of wild nights in my city. It was a fun game while it lasted, and it lasted a while, until I got pregnant.

My difficulty was finding the father. Or "donor," since "father" was a bit of stretch.

My friends advised me to let it go. "What if he wants to keep the baby? What if his girlfriend thinks she should be Mom?"

"That's what lawyers are for," I said, waving a sheaf of documents. Of course I had my worries, too, but curiosity won out. It wasn't that I wanted a partner or co-parent; I just wondered which one he was.

One of them looked sexy in dresses.

One of them had just started T.

One of them was so bland that I'd forgotten all detail.

One of them took pictures. When I found out, I stole his phone.

Little Davy was born at two in the morning. Right away he was my favorite creature on the planet, the most beautiful and perfect breather ever to breathe. I wanted to lick his eyeballs. I wanted to gnaw on the cord with my teeth. His head was covered in downy silver, a bump on his forehead the size of a pea.

A few weeks after Davy was born I sent out a mass email to all the couples I'd fucked:

> *Dear Friends,*
> *Hello! I hope you remember me. I definitely remember you!*
> *I'm searching for the identity of my child's father. Were you my*
> *lover between 3/13–3/27? If so, please contact me on the confidential*
> *voicemail number below.*
> *Sincerely,*
> *Cassie (and Davy)*

Then I waited. Then I forgot.

Davy smelled like sourdough bread with jam; Davy's hair was iridescent; Davy's hooves clattered on the kitchen floor when he practiced standing: knobby legs bent, sliding into the splits. Soon he was walking delicately on a leash for our trips to the park.

It was at the park that I first noticed the old school sedan with an old school driver. He took shots of my porch, made notes in a book. I watched from behind the pirate ship on the playground. Usually he left after half an hour, but one afternoon he stayed and stayed.

Davy and I played hide-and-seek. We played kickball, ran races, cantered the park. Davy nuzzled my knapsack, searching for hay. It was time to go home, time for snacks and a nap.

We walked past the sedan. It was only creepy for a second,
but that second was long.

"What do you want?" My keys in my fist.

He handed me a letter, becoming a minor character.

Shaking, I shepherded Davy inside, fed him apples and oats,
let him sleep on the couch.

Violet envelope. Red ink on pink paper. It smelled like sourdough bread with jam. Signed *Love, Veronica*. A name I could taste.
The memorable girlfriend of the unmemorable man.

I could barely see the rest of the letter, could only scan it
for phrases: *custody agreement* or *rightfully mine*. Neither appeared.
Instead I saw *pleasantly surprised* and *if you don't mind*. I saw *at your
convenience*.

I stared at the bottom of the letter again. *Love, Veronica*. Then
I read it from the top.

She wanted to meet Davy. Her boyfriend, she said, needn't
be involved.

The more I thought about it, the more sense it made. She'd
had large front teeth, thin lips, a patch of platinum hair that went
all the way down the middle of her back. She'd worn high heels.
I'd straddled her, though I don't usually do that. The thing about
being in high demand is you get to choose what you want to do, and
who you want to do it to, but Veronica had me acting like somebody
else. I thought maybe I'd discovered a new side of myself, but then
I only wanted to do those things with her.

I told Davy that a friend was coming to meet him. I brushed
his hair and braided his tail. He could tell I was nervous; he

wouldn't leave my side all morning as I dressed and re-dressed, trying to find a balance of outfit between *mom* and *third*. When he nuzzled my arm, I just let him. Being around Davy kept me calm when nothing else did.

The hour arrived when Veronica was due, and Davy and I sat on our couch staring at the front door, a couple of abandoned toys on the floor between us. The house was spotless. Davy was perfect. I was a mess. If I'd had a cigarette, I would've smoked it. I'd decided on hippie mom, jeans and an airy blouse, and was regretting my choice. Remembering the sedan and wishing I'd gone with business casual. Remembering her heels.

Davy scratched a hoof against the wood floor.

"Could you stop doing that?" I said.

He stopped. She arrived.

I could tell right away there was chemistry between them. I want to say the bump on Davy's head grew from the moment he met her, but I could be imagining that. She was my worst fear and highest hope rolled into one: more like him than I could ever be.

When I opened the door, Veronica kissed my hand, something she'd done during our night together, while Davy peeked from behind my leg. "He has your eyes," she whispered to me. Then she bent at the knee and held out a hand for Davy to sniff. He looked at me, and I nodded. I even pushed him forward a little. I liked her, and I wanted to make a good impression.

"He's lovely," she said. Then she looked at Davy and said, "You're lovely."

Davy puffed into her hand. He nudged it, drawing her into the house.

"Sorry," I said. "Won't you come in?"

We sat on couches, saying nothing. Veronica turned down tea and fed her cookies to Davy. I could tell she was working up to something, so I just let her.

"I'd love to have Davy over to meet my other boys," she said finally.

"Other boys?" I tried to remember her house, tried to picture a toy chest shoved in the corner of the dark room, or maybe the faint smell of hay.

"They're dying to meet you," she said to Davy. He didn't have many playmates, or any at all, really. So far he seemed content to play board games with me, to run around in the park, to entertain himself with make believe. But it wouldn't last. I knew that. How long before I wasn't enough? How long before I should be worried if I was?

Davy batted his velvety eyes at me, begging. "That would be nice," I said. "Other boys."

"Oh, Davy." Veronica held up her hands, and seeing them made me salivate. "You will be a celebrity."

Davy blushed. I'd never seen him do that. I noticed that the bump on his forehead had grown. I don't know that anyone but a mother would've caught it, but I did. It'd changed shape, gone from round to conical. I didn't want to embarrass him, so I didn't say anything. When I looked up, Veronica was staring at me. She winked, and it seemed like suddenly there was a breeze from nowhere blowing down my shirt.

"Tonight," Veronica said. "I'll send a car for Davy."

"Okay," I said. And once again, she had me doing things I wouldn't normally do.

○

The first time, Davy came home glowing.

The second, he had glitter in his mane.

The third, the tip of his horn had poked through the skin, and someone had drawn a bull's eye around it.

The fourth, someone replaced the bull's eye with a rainbow.

The fifth evening he was late. I called Veronica's number, but no one answered. I paced the living room, startling at every car that drove by, watching headlights sweep up my ceiling as it grew dark. Finally one stopped. I opened the door and saw a limo parked out front, Davy's head coming through the sunroof. He whinnied when he saw me, then came trotting daintily up the walk. He had a dozen strands of beads around his neck and smelled like cologne. I charged out to the limo and pounded on the window.

Inside: boys with orange hair and tight shirts, boys with hair hanging in their faces, boys with neon bracelets and sunglasses. The car was full of boys and boys.

"Who are you?" the boy who rolled down the window said.

"I'm Davy's mother," I said. "Where's Veronica?"

"Oh my god," the boy said. "We love Davy!"

They all began to cheer. Someone turned up the music, the bass rattling the doorframe.

"I thought that other lady was his mom," one of the boys said. Then they rolled up the window. The limo drove off.

I ushered Davy into the house. His horn was almost all the way grown now, and sharp, too. He kept tossing his head and narrowly missing me with it as we went inside. Embarrassed. Angry. But so was I. I'd just began my lecture when the phone rang.

"Apologies," Veronica said. "It'll never happen again."

"Can we talk?" I said.

"I'll come," she said.

Davy was in bed when she arrived. She kissed my hand.

"I'll defer to your judgment," she said on the couch. "He's your son."

She smelled so good I wanted to eat her. We kissed on the mouth, and I straddled her legs. "Our son," I said, though I hadn't planned on saying that and, later, wished that I had not.

I loved Davy. I feared for Davy. I did not know what they wanted with him. And I missed our days in the park, just the two of us.

I followed them. Sometimes they went back to Veronica's house and disappeared inside. Sometimes they went dancing. Sometimes they swam naked in the lake, and sometimes they went for milkshakes. Wherever they went, Davy was surrounded. They were always petting his hair and touching his skin, feeding him treats, dressing him up. He let them lead him around. They spoke to each other, but he spoke to no one. He was beautiful and mute. Placid. A dullness to his eyes that had been masked by the growth of his horn.

I didn't tell him what I'd seen, but at home I pleaded with him: "I love you no matter what," I said, "but you have to stand up for yourself."

He arched his smooth neck, blinked slowly. I detected a trace of mascara.

"You're more than your looks," I said, but Davy was already rolling his eyes.

That night, I climbed into bed with him, something I hadn't done since he was small. Underneath the cologne, I could still catch whiffs of sourdough. I held him to my body, his hair brittle from being dyed, his smooth coat gone coarse. He thrashed around during the night, fighting something in his dreams, so much that I was forced to leave or risk being impaled on his horn.

I got him a math tutor. I sent him for horn lessons. I bought him Spanish language tapes and a subscription to National Geographic magazine. I signed him up for soccer.

He wouldn't even put on his shin guards. He shredded the magazines and threatened the tutor with his horn.

"That's it," I said. "It's coming off."

I laid out my implements: scissors and a saw.

That evening, Davy didn't come home at all. He was gone one, then two, then three days before the black sedan showed up again. I ripped up the letter without reading it.

She wouldn't win in court. I was Davy's mother, and I'd raised him right, and I had the right look: blonde and big-breasted, and I could cry on command. I could get what I wanted from cops and judges. The morning of the hearing, I painted my nails. I curled my hair. I stood in front of my closet, looking at the things I'd worn on dates and the things I'd worn underneath. Weighing what it would take to get Davy back.

With Jellyfish

A girl swims in the sea at sunset. Her mother tells her not to, and the girl tries not to, but she does it anyway. She does it for the buoyancy. She does it because she's not supposed to.

The sea is exactly the same temperature as her body. She floats on her back, watching the sky flicker. She feels a prick on the back of her arm, and when she looks down, the water is full of tiny jellyfish no bigger than her pinky. The girl holds very still and waits for the waves to wash her closer to shore.

Now you've done it, her mother says when the girl returns home.

How did you know? But as soon as the girl says it, she feels an itch on her arm. A pebble of gray skin like a wart flakes off, a spot of blood in its place. The girl grimaces.

You just killed one, her mother says.

The girl's skin dries. She can tell when a baby is forming because a small, round patch goes whiter and whiter until it bubbles out like a boil. Sometimes half a dozen form simultaneously across her limbs and torso, and her mother calls it an outbreak. Sometimes only one, and her mother sarcastically calls it a baby.

Her mother says things like, *I hope you don't eat your babies.*

She says things like, *You wouldn't understand since your kind don't raise their young.*

After the boil forms, the new head turns rubbery and thin. The threadlike tentacles appear while it is still attached. She is immune to their sting, but her mother is not. The jellies stay active for an hour or more after they drop from her body, so she tries to be careful about where they land. She tries to clean up after herself. But she doesn't always notice when it happens.

Ouch, her mother says. *Right on my chair? You did that on purpose.*

Some of them she saves to feed to the bad kids at school. The ones who call her names or disrupt class. She needs quiet to focus during social studies or she can't pass the quizzes. She keeps dropped jellies in a plastic sandwich bag in her backpack. They are so small she can slip them into an open milk carton. The bad kids get terrible stinging rashes and are sent home.

Now she can swim in the sea whenever she wants. Her mother shoos her out every evening, tells her it's for her own good. In the water, she can feel her skin drinking. The jellies turn her phosphorescent. All night she strokes, and her arms leave light trails in the water. She sees other sea life, but even the dangerous ones are afraid of her. She is perfectly safe with her babies. Sometimes they drop in the water, which makes her happy because she knows they will live.

One is born with eyes. It forms differently than the others, burrowing in instead of ballooning out. When it drops—or rather, when it pushes itself from her body—it leaves a quarter-sized hole in her forearm, several inches deep. There is no blood. Just a piece of her gone. The jelly lands on the carpet without a sound. She watches two dark areas near the top, thinking that they look like eyes. She leans closer, and they contract like pupils.

She moves to the left, and they shift to follow.

She doesn't tell her mom about the one with eyes. It's weeks before another begins to burrow. This time she races to the water, hoping it won't drop on asphalt and shrivel, hoping it will wait for waves to be born. She almost makes it, but a car pulls up in front of the boardwalk. A few of the kids from school climb out.

Look, it's the jellyfish girl. Her arms are disgusting.

I bet she has herpes.

I bet she has AIDS.

They play keep away with her backpack until one of the pretty girls touches her hair.

Jelly's not so bad. Her haircut's cute.

Suddenly they're laughing again. She feels air on her chest, feels something undone. The pretty girl has untied her bikini; she's standing there topless while the cool kids laugh.

In this manner she loses another baby.

O

Now the cool kids call her *Jelly*. They smear her locker with blood-colored jam. In the lunchroom they trip her, so she drops her tray. A boy steals her cell phone and sexts all her contacts: Mom, Doctor, Dentist, Neighbor Two Houses Down.

She knows she knows something, but she doesn't know what.

Her mother says things like, *I hope you don't beat your babies.*

She says things like, *You wouldn't understand since your kind fuck so young.*

O

There's a boy at school with dark brown eyes who watches when she drops her tray. One day she's in the bathroom crying when she hears her name.

Jane.

He's standing by the sink, looking out the window. *Let's go,* he says.

They cut class, walk outside past the bleachers. They walk into the woods and she isn't afraid.

Beyond the woods is the beach and her jellyfish, swimming.

How did it happen?

She tries to explain.

O

When the baby starts to come, she's alone. Her mom's shopping. She's just watching TV. She knows why she's wet, knows body from ocean. The boy has a car. She texts him; he comes.

The hospital races to glow in her window. He's holding her arm; he's saying her name. They're inside and she's trying to explain to the doctors that it's a jellyfish baby. She went swimming and she felt the sting. The ocean did this, with its sea foam swirls.

She holds out her arm, shows the burrowing world.

When she wakes up, she's burning. The boy's asleep by her bed. He's snoring, slumped. She wants him to wake up. The heat in her arms starts crying and nuzzling. It has eyes this time; mouth a jam-colored O.

The boy wakes up. *What will you call her?*

Aurelia, she says, and just like that her jellyfish baby has a human girl's name.

In two days she'll go home with the boy. The boy's mother will sing Aurelia to sleep. The boy's mother will call Jane's mother and try to talk sense, but her mom will hang up.

Back at school, the kids will avoid her. Boy by her side, Aurelia home with his mom. Her arms will be smooth. She'll dream of the sea. But they live inland, Great Plains. She's never seen the ocean wave.

With Replica

She had these toys, my daughter, like action figures but animals instead of super heroes. A bald eagle with outstretched wings. An African dog. A meerkat litter on hind legs, stuck to the same plot of plastic land. They didn't start out as a collection, but that's what they became. When asked what she wanted for her third, fourth birthdays, it was an easy answer. I appreciated the gender neutrality of animals. Clydesdales, not ponies. Jackrabbits and grizzlies, not bunnies and teddies.

It mattered because of my son. Dylan. He was two years older, born breach. From the beginning, he did things the hard way. Like me: the kids' dad had been two vials of frozen, so it was my midwife holding my hand while the surgeons sliced me open below the curtain. Afterward, while I'd been busy refusing blue blankets and sports-themed nursery décor—and asking why every boy's onesie had to have an emergency vehicle on it—he'd been busy turning the tables on me. I sent him to preschool in the purple pants he loved and loudly lectured every three-year-old who said boo to him about it. "Purple," I said, "belongs to everyone." When my son asked Santa Claus for a Barbie, I relented. When he refused to let me cut the bangs that'd grown over his eyes, I picked my battles. But when he wanted the toy makeup kit, when he asked for everything in pink pink pink, when he demanded the ponies and bunnies and teddies, I lost my resolve. I cut him off.

I wouldn't turn my daughter into a princess; why would I do it to my son?

And like any thwarted princess, he was pissed.

He moped around in the solid green and yellow t-shirts I insisted both kids wear, the brandless, adjustable-waist pants. He scowled from below the bowl cut—not long, not short—I gave them both. He drew elaborate tattoos on his hands with pen, barbed wire and thorns. He hunkered down in the basement to watch age-inappropriate medical reality shows, one after the other. Extreme Plastic Surgery, and Hospital Horrors.

"You kids are getting lazy," I said and signed them both up for soccer.

While they were at practice, I picked up an extra shift at Raggedy Riches, a consignment store that traded beat-up exersaucers for vintage high chairs, and where I spent the day hanging clothes for girls on one side of the store and boys on the other. Maddening, but the employee discounts were great. Money was tight; the two vials of frozen that worked had been preceded by seven vials that didn't, each round going on plastic until I'd maxed out three cards. I'd stopped paying two of three. My phone rang all day long.

It was easy, at work, to pick up soccer cleats. There were so many piles of clothes around all the time, it was easy to set aside a winter coat, a pair of rain boots. The strollers were parked right out front. It was easy to stash one around the corner by the dumpster, to be picked up after work. Easy, too, when the box of animal replicas came in, to transfer the toys to a shopping bag and fill the box with someone else's clothes.

"Look," I said when we were all home after practice, Dylan sulking in shin guards. I dumped the shopping bag onto the floor: a toucan with a berry in its beak, a flying squirrel, a red-eyed tree frog. A whole pile of them that Jules, my daughter, immediately set to organizing. This was how she played. She stood them in categories—forest animals, jungle animals—and then, when she was done, changed the categories—vertebrates, invertebrates. She never made them talk or hoot or roar. There was no plot to her playing. Just infinite methods of categorization.

Dylan picked up one animal and then another, turning them over, studying them. "How come we don't have real toys?" he said.

I pulled a container of eggs from the fridge to start dinner. We ate a lot of eggs. "What's not real about these?"

"For one thing, the cows don't have udders," he said, holding one up to show me.

I studied it, too. He was right.

"What's the other thing?" I said.

"The other thing is that these toys suck," he said.

I gave the cow to Jules, and she set it next to a flamingo. I watched her for a while before asking about the category.

"Normals," she pointed to a mountain goat and wild boar, "and weirds." The red-eyed frog, the udderless cow.

Dylan swept her piles together. "They're all weird," he said.

Jules went right back to organizing. Dylan left the room. I scrambled the eggs and put them in the pan.

If Dylan had been the one to come home with the new animals, I wouldn't have been concerned. I expected his anger; I expected him to be bullied. I was ready to fight him, and I was ready to defend him. I would lay down my life to support his right to be who he was, but I'd be damned if I'd let him be a stereotype. This was the push and pull of daily life with Dylan. So if he'd shown up with a melted half-hyena, half-peacock in his bag, I would've punished him for destroying his toys and ordered a heart-to-heart about gender conformity and the value of a dollar. "Do you know how much those toys cost?" I would've asked, though I didn't know the answer.

Instead, the mismatched animal parts started showing up in Jules's backpack, and she acted just as surprised as I was to see them there. "Cool," she said the first day, lifting the hyena-peacock and squinting at it. "Whoa," she said the second, holding an elephant's body with the melted-on heads of a tyrannosaurus, a cobra, and an okapi. "Mom, look," she said the third day, and showed me a winged jellyfish.

I watched Dylan closely.

I checked the house for lighters.

But I didn't ever remember us having a jellyfish.

On the fourth day, Jules stashed her backpack under her bed. Acted sick, without the fever. Shrugged me off when I asked about school. I sent her down to the basement with snacks and Dylan, to watch Flu Bachelor and The Uninsured.

While they were in the basement, I went through her backpack. The ubiquitous replica was wrapped in a towel. I expected half-lion, half-armadillo. Half-loris, half-tapir, with a daub of glass frog.

Instead half-test tube, dotted with doll head.

Half-vial, half-girl.

Half-dad, half-mom.

First I talked to Jules, then Dylan, then their teachers, then the vice-principal. The vice-principal stared at me over his desk. Raised his eyebrows when I described the replicas.

"Has Jules been tested for autism?"

"This isn't about Jules. This is about someone doing something weird to my kid. Bullying, that's what it is."

Mr. Fletcher picked up a pencil sharper shaped like a dachshund. "Inanimate objects don't bully children. Children bully children. I've seen plenty of bullying, and this doesn't qualify. I'd say you're the proud parent of a daughter with an overactive imagination."

"I'll sue," I said. We both knew I was lying.

That night television voices whispered from beneath the floorboards. We ate breakfast for dinner, mouse head pancakes with butter and syrup.

"Kaitlyn Binkle says we should be a gluten free household." Jules speared a mouse ear with her fork. "She says gluten smears up your guts like paste."

"Kaitlyn Binkle is a coconut crab."

"Dylan! Don't be mean."

"I'm not. Coconut crabs are cool. Kaitlyn can hang off the climbing wall for a really long time."

Jules poured syrup on her fingers and smeared it on her lips. "Lipstick."

While I was trying to decide whether to tell her that lipstick was tested on bunny rabbits and that she could grow up to be either a doctor or a firefighter, Dylan smeared syrup on his lips, too.

"Boys don't wear lipstick."

"It's not lipstick, it's food." Dylan pushed his chair away from the table, then dropped a crumpled piece of paper on my plate. "Hey Mom, I forgot to give you this." Both kids disappeared down the basement stairs. I sat at the table smoothing pink paper. In perfect cursive:

> *Dear Beatrice,*
> *I miss you.*
> *Faithfully,*
> *Faith*

Faith-Loretta had perfect handwriting. She had perfect lips and perfect breasts that swayed when I fucked her from behind on all fours. We both wanted children and picked a donor together, but before I got pregnant God showed up at our door.

God was otherwise known as Harlan, head of a megachurch sprawled in Spokane. He'd disowned his daughter when we moved in together. Kicked her out of their church, said she'd never been born.

Six years later he knocked on our door—the father who'd said she was dead to her family. We both hoped he'd found PFLAG or a compassionate God.

"He has to apologize. To you and me both."

Harlan stood on our stoop, hat in hand, eyes averted. His daughter half-in, half-out of the frame. She missed her mother, six sisters and brothers. She missed Nine Mile Falls and the hymns from their church.

After Harlan drove off in his truck Loretta went into the bathroom and ran the tub. She stayed inside a long time, not taking a bath. That night I helped her pack a bag.

"Just a long weekend," she said, "to see if they've changed."

I waved from the driveway as she drove off in her truck. That night I made frozen pizza and watched TV for hours. She called around midnight. "I've got new nieces and nephews. They're cute and they love me. I'm so glad I came."

The next night she missed me, and the night after that.

"We did house rounds today. You know, neighbors in need."

The next time she called, I heard songs in the background. "Rachel's on piano and John's on guitar."

A week went by.

"I've got things to take care of. My mom needs me on Friday. I'll come home after that."

Saturday, Sunday. She called Tuesday night.

"We sang the night's prayers. Even the kids."

Two more weeks and her mailbox was full. I drove to Spokane in a blur of unease. Calvary Star Covenant of Abundant Fellowship took up an entire block surrounded by asphalt. Hundreds, maybe thousands of cars circled a long row of double doors, each set divided with a cross down the middle.

"Loretta," I mumbled, "what have you gotten yourself into?"

Inside the lobby there were brochures and water fountains and free coffee and two middle-aged ladies with bouffant hair in green uniforms sitting behind a green-and-gold desk.

"May I help you?"

"I'm looking for Loretta Almgren."

"Pastor Almgren's daughter?"

"His oldest."

"Of course. She's probably home cooking with her mother right now. She's come back to the fold. Baptized last Sunday."

Turns out Loretta was missing, all right. She took the name Faith when she went underwater. A few weeks with her family and she was reborn. Our commitments unsealed, our history rewritten. Loretta was gone, replaced by Faith, who sent Christmas cards signed *Your sister in Christ*.

While I was grieving I bought the first of the vials. If I wanted a child, I'd have to do it myself. Five vials in and I was pregnant with Dylan. Four vials later I was pregnant with Jules.

By the time I realized I needed a lawyer, I had two young children and a custody suit. Loretta who'd wanted a baby was dead, replaced by Faith, who believed in the devil. Her lawyer stalked me and discovered my kids. Traced the vials to our joint account. It never occurred to me to split up on paper, since our commitment ceremony wasn't legally binding. I'd paid for the vials with credit cards linked to an account under both of our names. Her lawyer claimed the vials were joint property.

Half-Dylan, half-Jules.

My whole heart froze.

And so in the middle of the night we moved. I stuffed what I could into garbage bags, strapped the kids in their car seats, and took off down the highway. Picked a small town when gas money gave out. Took the first job that would have me, Raggedy.

Faith was a stranger. I missed Loretta. She'd been bitten by a dog when she was ten. The wound healed into a scar, quiet until I found it. Subtle, the difference between damage and skin.

That night I asked Dylan where he'd gotten the letter.

"Faith gave it to me. That lady who visits."

"Does she visit your school?"

"After school on the playground."

"Sweetie, you aren't allowed to talk to strangers."

"Faith's not a stranger. She's friends with Jules, too. She has hair down to her butt and wears long skirts all the time."

Jules piped up. "She gave Dylan a pink t-shirt. He's hiding it under his bed. It's the kind you won't let him wear."

"Shut up, Jules. You promised Faith not to tell."

"But you got a shirt and I didn't."

"She gives you stuff all the time."

There are Bible stories about splitting a baby, King Solomon's wisdom undoing a thief. A week later Faith showed up on our stoop in a long denim skirt, her hair wrapped tightly around her head in twin braids. She sat on the sofa, arranging her skirt like a blanket. Then she started to cry.

I sat on the other end of the sofa, which was how our relationship had started years ago in college.

"Does anyone from church know you're here?"

"No. I told them I was visiting Aunt Kay."

The house darkened around us, music rising from the basement. I wanted to say her name, but wasn't sure which name to say.

With Me

I wasn't what you wanted, but I was what you got.

You wanted a charming brown-eyed child who never threw tantrums in the cereal aisle; you wanted a bookworm or a soccer star. You wanted a child that looked like your husband. You'd been *so careful* about your indiscretions. Condoms with the mountain biker; condoms with the bi-curious couple; condoms with the barista. What I came out different, you thought you were busted. But I was different-different. More than a pinprick hole in a condom. I came from your body, and I came from a lab.

The doctors explained while you sat in shock, trying to nurse what was wrapped in the blanket. They spoke softly. Someone shut the door. *Not the first* and *Where do you work?* When they found out you worked for GenTech the room got quiet. Dad started to cry.

In time you saw lab animals differently. Each one was me, heart quickened in fear.

You came home smelling of white coats and witness, anonymous mice designed for your lab. You worked in the lab, and you slept in the lab, and you brought home animals before they died of The Sick. You substituted healthy for damaged. *Our secret*, you said. *No one will know.*

After a few years you couldn't keep all the lab animals. The basement and attic were full of sharp teeth. So you started a habit of clandestine visits: old growth forests, ghost beaches, high dunes. Sometimes Dad went with you at night. Loaded the truck with cages, with claws. You drove for hours, scrambling animal compasses. Unloosed the cages under swathes of thick trees.

In dreams I saw their backwards feet.

At home you called it my *little house*. But on the phone to the doctor I heard you say *cage*. Sometimes on weekends a circuitous maze, long hallways tangled, dead ends and stale cheese. One Halloween you dressed as a cat. I heard you laughing from the faraway house. Ran on my wheel until your truck pulled away. Slept in wood chips, carrot for teat.

Sometimes you told me I had beautiful eyes. Cradled me, stroked the fur on my belly.

Sometimes you yelled or set my wheel spinning. Threatened to take me back to the lab.

Over time I learned how to tilt the latch and press against the door of the little house until it opened. I was careful not to use this trick too often. I needed you to think I was stupid, that the slit in the door was your mistake.

O

Homeschooling was the obvious choice.

I learned your language as fast as any animal. But although I spoke, words never felt natural. Instead I nipped expressively, rubbed my face against doorways.

You stopped giving parties. Sometimes you didn't come home.

When you didn't come home it was me and Dad. He'd swear me to secrecy, unhook the latch. We'd turn on the radio, cook grilled cheese with butter. Dad never put my food in a maze or shocked my feet when I turned the wrong corner. Dad called me by name, walked me off-leash. Read to me about Life In The Wild.

He said I was the perfect child. My red eyes red in photos, red in darkness when I led him through deserted streets, showing him the world I knew on instinct. Like teaching him to drive; I wanted him to know the route I knew. Smells, dirt brushing underfoot.

Once, he slept on the couch; let me inhabit the bed, your bed. I burrowed down into the softest feeling. Different from wood chips, burlap, scraps.

I knew about the others, the ones you'd loosed in woods, in water. They spoke to me, a vibrating frequency; tremor and startle, electric with trouble.

O

A little older, and I asked for a pet.

You stroked my head. Dad smiled, seeing us this way: your gentle side, the side you showed him.

After that you called me *Pet*.

A little older, and I asked for a playmate. A sister, brother, kid next door. That night you talked it over, voices like cream on the surface of my night. In the morning you smiled, dressed me to go out. We drove past shops and pastel children. Past a church, dogwoods in bloom. The warehouse stood on gravel and a scruffy little lawn. Pictures of animals decorated the building. We walked inside, and I heard the noise: barking, gnawing, clawing, tomb. You wanted me to choose a sibling. I could set one captive free. I swerved away from dogs into the cat room, but all that licking, and the catnip mice. Rabbits came in pairs, but you said just one. To the dogs again.

I closed my eyes and spun.

I called her *Sister* and *Friend* and *Happy*, but that was wishful thinking. Her cage was bigger and barer. She was always in search of something to chew, and her words, when she tried them, were garbled with bone. Her maze was an electric fence that made her fear the ground. She peed in corners and on her own bedding, and there was more information in the scent of her urine than her language. It reeked of history, of street fights and cells, but when I tried to speak to her of captivity, she scoffed and said I knew nothing. "You, fucking wheel," she slurred, lip curled over a *treat*, dried slaughterhouse remains. "Run run sleep." She rolled her eyes and drooled.

You crawled around the house with rag and cleaner, sniffing the carpet. I wouldn't say I was sad to see the dog go.

There was a recovery period, something like mourning—not for my lost sibling, exactly, as for the failed experiment. You didn't like failed experiments. Your career was results-oriented. There was a whole week when you didn't come home. You spoke tenderly on the phone, asked me what I was reading. Dad and I hunkered down, waiting on your decision.

Then you were back, in my room one night, billowing foreign smells. You lay on the floor on your back next to the little house. I breathed through my mouth so as not to learn too much, but even then I could taste sadness all over you: the animals you'd treated, the humans you'd handled. I choked on it. I didn't understand how you could walk around like that, how you could lay there breathing in and out, whispering to me, without gagging on the smell.

I learned too much that night, though I didn't hear anything you said. So it was as much a surprise to me as to Dad when my new sibling showed up. This one all your own.

Of your body. Of the lab.

But nothing at all like me.

I tried not to think in terms like *more* and *better*. More human. Better toys. She got to wear clothes and watch videos. She got a sitter when you went to work, and the sitter was afraid of me. Even Dad couldn't help laughing when she made the sign for *tickle*, though he always caught himself, gave me a sympathetic look. She wore diapers and ribbons. She liked to show off by climbing the maple tree out back and swinging one-handed.

She was allowed outside more. I watched from the window, pretending to read. It didn't matter anymore how often I lifted the latch.

When you spoke on the phone, you laughed about how easy your first was, but you said it in a way that suggested you preferred a challenge.

I called her *Beast* and *Animal* and *Freak*.

You had to keep us separated.

I ran away, but the streets were ugly and fierce without Dad, the woods foreboding. I slipped back inside, where my sibling was snoring. I watched her giant hands twitch and fist. I wondered if I could lure her away. If I could entice her to the faraway trees. I couldn't sign well, but I knew enough to say, *Follow. Out.* You'd raised me on mazes, raised me to be smarter than I'd been at problem-solving.

Back out, to the lab. I'd never been there, but I followed your scent the whole way. Smells of death and wrong. The sizzle of panic, and of mutation, everything inside out, twisted messages and non-sense. They could not cry for help. They could not comprehend not-pain or read their own labels.

In another area, silence. The ache of waiting.

The Sick Ones chattered insanely as I climbed up to examine the vials and dishes and powders. *Thing Not-Caged,* they said. *Will fall, will die, will eat the terrible.* Some of them couldn't stop laughing; some repeated the same phrases. *Feed!* they screamed. *Open door!*

I opened all their cages. They raced around the room, out the door, into the street. I left with my vial, but I'd lost heart. At home I kept it buried in wood chips until I finally just threw it away.

When you got sick, we all waited with you for the results. But your years of research bought you exactly nothing. Maybe the cure was hiding in the woods or the water, buried in the bodies of those you'd freed. Maybe we were the contagion, me and my sister, your half-breed lab babies radiating disease.

Whatever the cause, it worked its quick damage, and you were gone.

You never asked for forgiveness.

We never granted it.

My sister and I stood together at your funeral, our father across the grave. Your other lovers peeping red-eyed from the small gathering. We talked about your life in a way that made it make sense. Not how you were, but how we wanted you to be.

Loving mother. Gentle soul. Brilliant scientist.

I smelled your body still putting out information. You were still working, still trying to tell us your story. I could tell that my sister noticed it, too. She touched my hand with her giant paw. It was our first touch.

Beast to beast.

With Spider

Sometimes she wished she were the mother of a normal child. Cleaning sticky off the counters at night or walking into a web on her way to the bathroom, Ella wished for a cooing, burping ball of human hair and teeth. She eyed other mothers in the grocery store, wondering if they knew. Their fat babies lolled in slings and baskets; their toddlers kicked shopping carts and screamed; their tweens and teens pretended not to know them. The other parents in her support group said they felt the same way, but in the grocery store she felt truly alone.

First grade had been the most difficult year. Ella was terrified that Spidie would vanish. Her therapist explained that anxiety was the body's warning sign, like a beeper going off; that she should pay attention to how she was feeling. Her therapist made her close her eyes and feel her heart beating: reckless, unread.

When Spidie came home from school, climbing delicately down the steps of the school bus, Ella smiled and asked her how her day went. But Spidie never confided secret crushes or what she'd eaten for lunch. Ella wondered if Spidie was popular, if the other kids bullied, if her teachers took care.

Sometimes (although she knew it was crazy) Ella still talked to Iris. She'd tell Iris silly things about her day, like which burrito she'd ordered for lunch or which songs she'd downloaded illegally at work. She imagined Iris laughing, making fun of her terrible taste in music. "Mom," Iris would say, "those bands aren't cool. Let me make you a playlist so you don't sound like a dork."

It had been two years, three months, and six days since the accident. Ella refused to talk about it or visit the corner where it happened. Refused to talk to her ex-husband or the parents who visited from Iris's school. She knew what had happened; she was just wishing. Talking to Iris was like controlling a dream. And she dreamed, too, but her dreams weren't for Iris. In dreams she held tighter, so her dreams were for her.

Ella knew it was early to adopt another child, but Spidie reached out to her. At first she was afraid she was unfit. If she couldn't keep a human child alive, how could she protect a spider? But Spidie was alone, and so was she. They stared at each other from across the room until finally Ella held out her sleeve. Spidie crawled onto it. They watched each other silently for a while, arachnid to person. They could be alone together, Ella thought. It was a perfect fit.

Their quiet, separate sounds—spinning, turning pages in a book—complimented each other.

How her day went: to be stuck in a desk was painful. She studied corners and branches. The threads built up inside her, made her spinnerets ache. Her legs shook. Her teeth were dry. At recess she climbed as high as the wall surrounding the playground and looked down at the normal children chucking their bodies across the monkey bars, sliding down slides on their backs. She didn't like to be on her back. For a spider, that was death. She'd tried to slide once but had accidentally thrown out a drop line. The next kid got tangled in her sticky and ran around swiping at his face and calling her bad names. She didn't go on the slide anymore, or the swings. She climbed as high as the wall but no higher because if she went higher she was afraid she wouldn't come back. And she couldn't do that to her mother. Her mother who loved her, in spite of it all.

Her secret crushes: in first through third grade, Spider Man because it was expected. In fifth, a boy who complimented her science project, a funnel-shaped web. In high school, the only other spider in her district, a badass older girl who refused to sit in desks or eat school lunches or *capitulate*, she said, *to the primate majority*. The school offered Spidie the same private lunchroom, where the older girl was already fang-deep in some anonymous bug. "Spidie," she said, licking blood. "That's cute. Your mommy name you that?"

What she ate for lunch: as she grew, so did her nutritional demands. She tried small mammals. Wrapped up rats. Drained birds. There was a door in the wall of the private lunchroom where she and the older girl set their refuse on a tray, wings and tails and eyeballs neatly packaged. She emerged from lunch feeling strong. And sometimes ashamed. The other kids didn't know for sure what went on behind the door of the private lunchroom, but they guessed. They edged away from her in the halls. No one asked her to prom.

O

Ella told Iris, "Today I ordered the spicy salsa. I don't know what came over me."

She told her therapist, "Sometimes I still hear her footsteps."

She told her support group, "Mine has been breaking curfew. I don't know what to do with her anymore."

When Spidie was home, Ella could think of nothing to say. *How was your day?* she asked over and over, as if repetition alone would change the outcome of the conversation.

Ella knew that adopting again was risky. Her support group warned her: jealousy, rage, acting out. Competition among species. But Ella was determined. A sibling would bring out Spidie's soft side. She was glad Spidie had found a friend, finally, but this other spider was wild. Her mother came to Ella's support group, sat in the back with her hands folded, nodded vigorously when people complained about their spider kids but never said much. Just the once, when she'd come in smelling of booze and blurted, "She gives me this *look*, and I'm like, what the hell, I'm not your *prey*. But they're hunters, right? Bloodsuckers. That's what they are, and that's what they'll always be."

Nobody said anything, and the woman had slumped back in her seat. In the support group, it was considered rude to talk about feeding. Everybody knew what spiders did. It wasn't necessary to dwell on it.

How her day was: she ate them still alive. In the park, after dark. She found them in the bathroom. She found them in the bushes. She snuck home with the taste of them still in her mouth.

Ella would go overseas to pick up her new daughter. She would name her Rose.

The night before her flight, she waited up for Spidie, heard her come in through the window. Spidie froze when Ella switched on the bedroom light.

"Are we okay, me and you?" Ella said.

Spidie wiped something from her mouth.

"This baby is for both of us," Ella said. "I want you to remember that. She's not a replacement."

Spidie nodded. It was as much acknowledgement as Ella had yet to receive from her. Spidie was too big for Ella's sleeve now, so Ella blew her a kiss. "I'll miss you," she said. "No parties while I'm gone."

In bed, trying to sleep, Ella dreamed of mixing formula and warming bottles. Of fat baby lips and tiny toes. All the things she'd missed, raising Spidie.

Spidie would be okay, she thought.

No, better. Spidie would be even better.

What she dreamed: fat baby lips and tiny toes. The things her mother wanted. "You going to eat it?" her friends said.

What she didn't tell her mother: she wasn't going to eat it. She was going to kiss its fat lips. And then she was going to leave her mother to her normal baby. She was going to be full and happy all the time.

With Stone Lion

The mean girls started it. Dragged Becky into the girls' bathroom and strapped a stone lion to her back. Left her lying sideways on subway tile, pregnant with statuary. Smoking and stalled I smelled their perfume. I unstrapped the lion, helped her straighten her dress. Without a word she fixed her hair and we walked into the lunchroom as if nothing had changed.

With Egg

Baby Egg was part of Taft's abstinence-only curriculum. Juniors were paired up, two to an egg. We had to pretend the egg was a baby, keep it from breaking or breaking the law. There were no substitutions; teachers tattooed our eggs in white ink. Which made it sound cool, except it wasn't. Taft needed condoms and a needle exchange.

The mean girls walked around in pairs, which was weird because they also bullied the gay girls. Gay guys they loved. Gave them blowjobs and talked about how their dicks tasted different. *If you dated girls we'd have babies by now!*

First I got paired with Cody Hawkins, but he stole a computer and set fire to the bleachers, so they sent him away to *relax* and *unwind*. Becky was Single Mom, so I asked Mrs. Temple if we could co-parent. I thought it'd be cool to do a second parent adoption, have a social worker sent to my house. Becky and I got into the drama, but Mrs. Temple made me Bereaved Mom, instead.

That night at dinner Dad asked me why I was dressed for a funeral.

I'm Bereaved Mom. I just lost my egg baby.

Dad's face got red, and Mom touched his shoulder. But I knew if they tried to help, the mean girls would destroy Becky and me both. So Becky and I took it into our own hands to raise a rogue baby egg into a chick.

We lived in the suburbs of suburbs of suburbs. Chickens weren't wandering the streets of Taft. So we drove to a sanctuary, past strip malls to Spackle. Becky had been there once with her mom.

We couldn't drive, which made driving more exciting. Becky borrowed her dead brother's car, and we took the back roads, skidding through dirt. When we got to Hoof Haven there were all these goats. Becky kissed me in front of a potbellied pig.

The people who ran the sanctuary were hippies, but also like Jesus with giant kind eyes. We explained that we were adoptive parents looking for a baby egg. The kind-eyed Jesus people looked at us lovingly. Offered us cider and an egg in an incubator.

We named the egg Jane, after my mom. We were supposed to rotate it three times a day. Becky wrote *X* and *O* in eyeliner, adding lashes to make *O* an eye. I slept over, and we stared at the incubator, telling ghost stories about demon chickens.

One by one the mean girls dropped their eggs: yolk on sandals, yolk on skirts. All we could think about was getting home from school to check on Jane. We took turns rotating *X*'s and *O*'s. We made up songs, lullabies for our bird.

We were sleeping curled up on Becky's futon when we heard something shaking, like cellophane crumpling.

We tiptoed to the incubator.

The top was off and the shell lay in shards.

Curled in the corner lay a hissing fit, ball of fur and fangs and claws.

That's not a chicken.

It looks like a leopard.

Jane arched her back and licked her paws.

Becky and I held hands, watching her. She was not what we'd expected, but she was ours, and we'd hatched her.

We were kind of scared. Kind of proud.

Kind of worried. Kind of glad.

We didn't tell anyone right away, not even our parents. We kept Jane at Becky's house because her mom didn't come home much anymore, and because it would've been impossible to hide anything in mine. Jane seemed like the kind of animal that needed milk, not feed, so Becky got a bottle at the grocery and we tipped it up to Jane's fuzzy mouth. She drank. She grew. She grew faster than we thought she should. Overnight she went from egg-sized to baseball-sized. Another night, and she looked like a regular kitten. Nobody was going to believe she'd come from our egg. They'd think we dropped it like everyone else.

But nobody was going to believe what happened next, anyway.

After three days of feeding our hatchling every time she mewed, I noticed two things: Jane had a definite preference for Becky over me, and she had sprouted what looked a lot like two tiny wings along her back. They were furry, though; unusable. *Decorative,* Becky said.

Becky slept in a dogpile of blankets underneath the table where we'd set Jane's incubator. She was up and down every two hours all night, warming bottles and feeding Jane. Every time I tried to take a shift, she lifted the bottle from my hands, patted my back, and said, *Get some rest.* So I did. My parents didn't like me staying over there so much—if they'd known her mom was gone, they wouldn't have let me at all—and especially on school nights, so when Sunday night rolled around, I went home. Slept in my own bed. Slept like a baby.

Monday, Becky wasn't at school.

The mean girls all had new eggs.

What I knew was that Glen's death was ruled a suicide. What I knew was that he'd gotten a mean girl pregnant, and instead of letting her get rid of it, the girl's parents had made an example out of her. But when the baby was born defective, they'd slipped away, pulling the girl out of school and disappearing with the baby. No forwarding address. Glen had tried to find them. Then he'd given up.

What I knew was that Becky had been the one to find him.

What I knew was that more than one person was responsible for Glen's death, but only person took the blame.

She'd been his favorite.

After school, I found Becky passed out on her pile of blankets. Jane wasn't there.

Psst, I whispered. I whistled as softly as I could. *Jane. Here, Janie.*

She bounded out from behind a sofa, her useless wings stretched out taut, but she froze when she saw me. Took two steps back. Hissed.

Come on, I said. *What's so wrong with me?*

Jane eyed me with suspicion. Then Becky twitched in her sleep, and Jane pounced on the blanket. Becky shrieked. *Bad girl*, she said, rubbing her ankle. She barely glanced at me. *All night she does this.* She showed me the scratches on her ankles. The small, round bruises on her calves.

You weren't at school, I said.

She shrugged. *What'd I miss?*

I told her about the new eggs, and how Mrs. Temple had paired people differently this time: everyone needed to be in a boy-girl couple, she said. No more joking around. No more dropping the eggs. The girls got felt pouches—blue or pink—to carry the egg, and a hook with our names where we left the pouches in the Health room at the end of the day. We got to watch educational videos while the boys went to Workplace Simulation instead of P.E.

So who'd you get? Becky said. She had dark circles under her eyes, and her hair was sticking up all over the place, and I wanted nothing more than to kiss her again. We hadn't kissed since the farm. She'd been so occupied with Jane that she hadn't eaten. I could smell the hunger on her breath.

I smashed mine, I said.

She smiled, which was what I'd been hoping for. *What'd Temple say?*

Workplace Simulation, I said. *I'm a janitor.*

She took my hand. I thought we might kiss then, but we didn't. *You've still got your first egg. You didn't tell them?*

I think we should show them, I said. *I think Jane should have some sisters.*

Jane hung her head out the back window, getting stares when we stopped for traffic lights. The hippie Jesus people still looked happy to see us, but they frowned at Becky. Offered her soup instead of cider. *How's the egg?* the man said while she ate. When she pointed at Jane hanging out the back window, he looked confused.

We need more, I said. *Lots more.*

The man gave Becky a long look and nodded. He disappeared and came back with a box full of eggs. He gave us a couple of bags of carrots, too, and some frozen hamburger patties.

We're getting rid of stuff, he said. *You came just in time.*

He stared at the back seat again.

You girls come back anytime, he said. *I mean it.*

The drive home was quiet, except for Jane yowling in the back.

Part of my janitorial job meant I had access to empty classrooms, so I plugged in the incubator and tucked it into a cupboard no one ever opened. Three times a day, I turned the eggs. The mean girls wore their pouches and watched their videos and nobody broke an egg. Mrs. Temple went around smiling, like she'd solved something. Like the point had been to turn us into successful parents, not prevent us from becoming parents in the first place.

I was furious. She didn't once ask where Becky was.

Becky was with Jane, who grew bigger and wilder by the day. The only part of her that wasn't growing was her wings. They stayed small and furry, silky to the touch. I wished they would grow big, carry her off. I wished Becky would come back to school. Jane played too rough with her, would leave ugly cuts on her arms. Whenever Jane saw me, she hissed and bristled. *She doesn't mean it*, Becky said, but it was almost like Becky was pleased that Jane didn't like me.

Maybe we should set her free, I said. *Maybe we should ask for help.*

Becky pulled a squirming Jane into her lap until Jane's swipes at her became too vicious. She let go, and Jane bounded across the room, knocking over a soda can and peeing right on the floor. Becky sighed and grabbed a bottle of cleaner.

She's mine, she said. *Don't you dare tell a soul.*

Instead of going over to Becky's, after school I hung around the Health room. Watching the incubator. Listening for the sound of cellophane crumpling. I told my parents I was working on a science project with Becky, and they seemed pleased about that. I didn't tell them I'd been made janitor. I didn't tell them about the new batch of eggs.

I had a feeling something would happen the night they hatched. I snuck out like I used to do to visit Becky, but instead went to school. I had a key for the building, and one for the supply closet. The Health room was open and humming. The closet door was shut, but from inside came the sound of tapping claws. Tiny hisses. For the first time, I started to worry about what all those miniature Janes would do to me once I opened the door without Becky there to protect me.

There was plenty of wire in the supply closet. I twisted a piece around the closet handle and ran it outside. I removed each egg from the pink and blue pouches hung on the wall. Then I shut the classroom door and pulled the wire.

Then I went home.

I didn't tell Becky.

The next morning, the whole school was bustling. I arrived late and was immediately intercepted by Mrs. Temple. *Young lady,* and the rest of her speech was drowned out by the crowd. She dragged me by the arm to the principle's office, and on the way we passed the Health classroom. A group of students were gathered around a large box on a table. One of the mean girls was lifting something out of it. I slowed, and Mrs. Temple dragged me harder. The girl looked back and me and smiled. In her hands was a chick.

As in, a baby chicken.

As in, not Jane.

No fur, no fangs. No sisters. No miracles.

Wings that worked.

Taft sent me away to *repent* and *shape up.* It wasn't for long— all I did was release some chicks—but my parents didn't let me return. When I went to say goodbye to Becky, she didn't answer the door. I looked in through the window, and the house was trashed, like maybe Jane had gone out of control or Becky's mom had come back. Her brother's car was gone, so I couldn't drive out to the farm in Spackle to see if she was there, incubating eggs that would hatch into fantasy because that was the story she wanted to tell.

With Cat

When I was a child, my mother bought me a Baby Mama doll. The doll was shaped like a human female with a hollow stomach. Inside her stomach was a silk-lined pouch; inside the pouch was a plastic Sweet Fetus. The fetus doll was supposed to teach girls that abortion was wrong, but I passed Sweet Fetus along to my brother. I don't know what my brother learned, what heartbeat or heartbreak when he swallowed the doll.

I put my freshman year abortion on my VISA card. My roommate paid for hers by giving blowjobs to the guy who got her pregnant. He was an RA in the Engineers' dorm. She charged $15 per, and the abortion was $250. A story problem for the SAT. When she'd earned the full amount he wrote her a check, then stuck it down his pants and made her beg. I'd like to say she broke his nose, but after the wedding they referred to sex as "trying."

We met at their wedding; I caught the bouquet. You slept with someone, bridesmaid or groom, but not with me. You were distracted, polite. A few years later we met at a grocery in a far away city, which felt like fate. You remembered my name, or a name like mine. I never corrected you, so it became my new name.

We stopped practicing SM while I was pregnant. I'd heard it could lead to a spontaneous abortion or litters of kittens.

While you were having an affair, you took your ring on and off. Sometimes you forgot to put it back on. Home disheveled, too late for late work, you'd stroke my hair ringless, shiny absence of promise.

I never stopped loving you best, but you loved her more. She had children, ten beautiful baby doll heads that bobbed in the window as you drove up. Or no children, not ever; or cats and tin cans. Or she was a man. I knew nothing of your second life, first life, or wife, whichever it was.

If you were going to make me into a monster, I'd go ahead and be monstrous. Give birth to a litter of sea snakes or dragons. Give birth to a child that loved guns and raw knives.

After you left, I melted all the jewelry you'd given me into a baby rattle for our little darling—girl child, yes, but not your girl.

Some guy on a plane. I traded for aisle. She had his mouth, or the mouth I remembered.

I fed our girl milk in a glass bowl. I carried her by the scruff of her neck. She yowled and hissed until I put my mouth over hers and drank her breath. After a while, that was the only thing that would stop her crying. I know how that sounds. You would not approve. I put a collar around her neck and wished you were there to see.

Or perhaps that was only what I'd wanted to do.

Or perhaps what I wished was to carry her inside me again. My prayer became: dissolve her. Dear god, shrink her into a pellet of bone and hair. Boil her down to crystals. Make her something I can hold in my mouth, a nugget smooth enough to swallow.

I tried to find you again. In other groceries. Other bodies. This time, when I got pregnant, I didn't hold back. I discovered that it's true, what I'd heard about the kittens.

I meant for you to stop me. I meant for you to come home. I thought there'd be some parameters in the world, a boundary the universe wouldn't let me cross. Her mouth licked pinkly, an animal of its own. She spoke in tongues. If I let it, I thought, that mouth would grow up naming names. Mommy. Monster. Blowjob. Baby.

You didn't stop me. God didn't either. But girls are harder to conceive than boys, and so it goes for death. Baby boys are fragile, more likely to die of prematurity and injury and SIDS. My girl just smiled at me from where I'd dunked her at the bottom of the tub, and after a while, I released my grip. She floated up to the surface, all forgiveness and air.

I will tell her that her sex saved her. It will be our private joke.

My girl and I are tight now. We are religious and hard. We are going to fight for justice and drown the kittens.

With Snakes

I.

Once a woman fell in love with a snake handler. She drove out to the country to visit him in a church that was a trailer. There were fire ants in the driveway, mannequins in the yard. The handler was the only one inside except for the snakes. His arms were covered in scars. The woman said, *I heard you teach people.* The handler nodded. He switched on an orange light so the woman would see the snakes sleeping in glass aquariums along the chapel walls. He took the woman's hand and touched it to the glass: pit viper, diamondback, cottonmouth, copperhead. At the end of the wall, he forced his hand inside an open tank and held it there until the snake struck. He showed her how to cut open the wound and suck out the poison. *The problem with most people*, he said, *is they don't know the right way to get bit.*

O

The problem with me, she said, *is that I've been bit before.* She showed him the fang marks on her back. Then she lifted a viper from its cage: *Like this?* She held the snake's head, stroked its body. The handler adjusted her grip. Offered her warm red wine and a spot on the pew. They laughed too hard, slanted into walls on the way to the bathroom. She asked if the lesson was over and didn't believe him when he said yes. Eventually she kissed him, and he kissed her back. Her pupils shrank to slits. Her tongue flicked into his mouth, and venom flowed into her teeth. She didn't bite; she didn't know if she could. He seemed kind enough, seemed like he knew what he was doing. When the babies came, he would protect them. Her, too, if she needed it.

She drove out every night, and every night they confessed. He told her he didn't believe in God. She told him her husband was in jail. They lay on the pews and talked until their bodies demanded more. Eventually he noticed her belly. She didn't confess how she thought there must be dozens in there, maybe a hundred. She didn't confess that they weren't his. She let him smile and murmur and rub her navel. She let him feel for a kick. She confessed that she had three children already. He told her he didn't believe in staying together for the kids.

She didn't like when the church people came in. Sunday mornings, Wednesday nights. They flung the snakes around, whooped and hollered, spoke in tongues. Their songs were okay. They called unborn babies acts of God, but hers were acts of nature.

Hers were acts of opportunity from the nice-enough guy at the bible study who wasn't the person she'd thought he was. Hers were a roiling ball of poison and perfection. Hers were hers, and she hid them from the church people by hanging back in the kitchen with the boxes of live mice. When the chapel was empty, she deposited a mouse—which she stunned by flicking the back of its head—in the cage of each weary snake.

2.

Once a man fell in love with a pair of snakeskin boots. In the dark of his closet he loved them in secret. The boots belonged to a God-talking man whose sermons slithered, whose arms were scarred. Both men kept their boots on in bed. Dirty heels scuffed sheets and bones. One night while the preacher was dreaming of hellfire the man pulled the boots off his lover's cold feet. In the morning, what could the preacher say? How protest theft in a down low life? Barefoot, he stumbled home to his woman. Gone fishing, he told her; waded into the water. Just like the parable of the alligator and the pickup truck, God told him to take off his boots, and cast them into the swamp.

You will be rewarded, he told his wife, in the Kingdom of Heaven.

She sat with her lap full of squirming mice. She knew she was supposed to stun them, drop them into the cage where snakes waited to swallow. But in dreams she slept with them, instead. Woke to a blanket of breathing mice, red eyes blinking, nuzzling, in love.

3.

Once a congregation fell in love with a sloughed-off snakeskin. Rumor had it this was no ordinary snake. A woman birthed it, then let it loose in her husband's bed when she found him lying with another man.

O

Thou shalt not, said the preacher. He was new to the fire and brimstone lifestyle. He'd come from the city, where they did things differently. He wore comfortable shoes and worked out at the gym.

O

Nights, the congregation gathered in the trailer and spoke in tongues with the voice of the snake. Lay on their bellies, slithered and teemed. When heat stunned them, they tore off their clothes. Come Easter they ground the snakeskin into powder, mixed it with whiskey, and passed the cup.

O

In the morning, when the city preacher arrived at the trailer, arms full of large print Bibles, he opened the door to a room full of snakes. *My God,* he said, *my soul's unclean.* He slammed the door, lay down on the driveway, and let fire ants write parables all over his body.

4.

Once a snake fell in love with a mouse, and spit him out.

O

Their eyes met.

O

What is a long life, thought the snake, compared to a moment of comfort shared with another creature?

O

The mouse thought of saints; of a nest he'd burrowed yesterday, or maybe today. The mouse wondered about time. How did it move? Did it taste like cheese? The mouse smelled bread baking in a trailer six towns away, and set off through the field.

With Squirrel

When we moved in, there was caution tape around the exterior of the building. The floors were destroyed, but the doors all shut tightly. The toilet flushing sounded like a baby. I was so heavy then, my body always becoming something else, a house or a weapon or a gamble or a gift.

Warning: pregnant women should not.

Our landlord, a white guy, asked if it'd just be us. By which he meant, no men. We'd fallen in love in the wrong place. Down the street in one direction was the projects. In the other, a Baptist church. So we called each other roommates and fucked in the dark. When the landlord came over, we shut the doors so he wouldn't see we only had one bed.

Should not: lift more than thirty pounds.

Breathe the fumes.

Handle explosives.

O

This was the house with the fridge that was hot to the touch.

This was the house with a couch and a pair of plastic legs in the backyard. We added leaves to the legs for pubic hair.

The neighbor played pop songs on a pipe organ.

I wanted to have a baby; you didn't.

O

We watched the baby through my shirt, listened to the neighbors listening through the walls. They complained about the noise. We picked our way across conversations that smelled like dynamite. I said, I can't do this alone. You said, This isn't working. Our teeth sizzled. Our tongues were cocked. The baby turned like a cartridge, over and over.

Warning: birth defects. Abnormalities. Syndromes.

Pay attention to the toxicity of the environment.

O

I won the argument, lost the baby. You put gigantic Christmas ornaments in the yard, and on them wrote, If stolen return to: They were something we owned. Someone stole the ornaments and Christmas treed our lawn. We woke to a forest of blunt trunks. Out back, squirrels nested in the plastic legs. Our cat got most of the babies, bringing them inside as gifts. They heaved their last breaths in your cupped hands.

Pay attention to: distress signals. Fetal kick counts. Blood pressure and protein levels.

To what isn't said. To what should be.

It matters what we call things. It's important to know whether the name is wrong, or the thing being named. We called each other roommates, and eventually you moved to the couch. You folded dollar bills into fish, stars, leaves. We put a window unit next to the hot fridge. The cat got eaten by an owl.

We stayed together, refusing to grow roots.

You brought the baby squirrels inside to raise yourself, curling around them on the couch. You nursed them, named them: Honey, Sweetheart, Cupcake. They gnawed on my hands in the night. I shooed them, swatted them. Tripped over and kicked them. Sometimes I still felt the flutters of life inside and forgot no one was there. Sometimes the feeling was a squirrel under the covers.

I said, What about rabies? I said, What about the baby?

The second one I lost was less far along.

The squirrel babies had squirrel babies. They fell out of cupboards, pillowcases, dresser drawers. They clung to your clothes. They swung from the curtains.

Reasons: chromosomal abnormality. Failure to properly implant. Maternal stress, as in a refugee camp or combat zone.

Squirrels nested in suitcases we packed in rages. You threatened to leave, then left, slamming the door, meaning the slam, taking it back too late.

I drove too fast in the pink lane; you slowed to a dangerous crawl in the blue. My skirt hissed lace. Bloodstains knocked on the door of my dress.

Pay attention to: an unlocked window. A skirt too loose around the waist.

I would've dressed my girl in sequined socks, my boy in clown pants. Stuffed twin hands in matching mittens. And triplets? Dyslexic, I turned 3 into 8, imagined 8 names starting with H: Holly, Hella, Hortense, Helga, Hanna, Hello, Ho-Ho, Help.

The third one I didn't lose.

Honey, Sweetheart, Cupcake, Mine.

But she wasn't mine. She was always yours, came out looking like you, tried to nurse your breast, fell asleep to your rocking. She screamed when I held her: Screamer, Scrappy, Squirrel. I imagined her onesie: Team Other Mom. You ambled the neighborhood, scooting the stroller over broken glass. She giggled at secrets you whispered in her tiny, perfect animal ears.

I wanted a baby that wanted me.

Instead my baby gazed up at you while I stood in shadow. Before I was scared you'd leave, but now I knew there was something worse. I gave birth and she left me for you.

I wallowed in my twice alone.

This was the house with the crooked crib.

This was the house with the corkscrew bottle.

Pregnant women should not: hate.

I tried to win you back with a winning smile, lipstick like a card trick. But you were busy with baby. You named her, but wouldn't tell me what. I called her Her. You laughed, and said that wasn't quite. The two of you smiled conspiratorially. You tattooed her name in invisible ink.

Can a baby bully? She loved you; how could I blame her? I'd loved you once, too.

○

I filed for divorce, meaning I took the couch. You slept with the baby on the bed we'd stolen. Attachment parenting, you said. Don't crush her, I said, and will you tell me her name?

Her name was Feral. She took after her mother.

Which mother, I asked.

Your gap-toothed grin.

The neighbors listened loudly, glasses cupped to paint peeling from walls that bled lead.

It took.

It took everything I had.

While you were busy with Feral, I herded squirrels into the attic. They sounded like a hurricane, claws scrabbling up and down walls. After a time I thought poison; I thought mercy. And Mercy should've been her name, but by then we weren't making decisions together. We named things, people, and gestures all on our own. We expected each other to guess the referent.

By then I had a baby tucked in my sleeve.

She looked like you, but I forgave her.

My girl was beautiful, all soft fur and bold brown eyes. Her tail swished when she nuzzled the bottle. People tried to tell me my baby was a squirrel, but people also told me that our love was unnatural.

With Killer Bees

I'm at the post office, in line, trying to mail a package for Mother's Day, when the pregnant lady two people in front of me just keels over. Everyone stands there for a minute, waiting to see if anyone's going to do anything, to see who will step up. No one does, so I shout, "Protect her head!" because that's something I've heard people say on TV. Still nobody moves, so I shove the guy in front of me out of the way and stand at the pregnant woman's feet. Her eyes are open. She's on her back with her knees in the air, wearing one of those awful jumpers women in late pregnancy sometimes wear, a jean skirt with overall straps and pockets with smiling sun patches sewn on. She looks me right in the eye and says, "They're coming."

"Who?" I say. I consider kneeling beside her, but something about the way she's staring at me, unblinking, keeps me on my feet.

Her resolve breaks for a moment, and her face tenses in fear. "I don't know what they'll do to me."

"Who?" I say again. I'm wondering what asshole knocked up a crazy lady and left her alone in a post office. She doesn't have a ring.

"The little ones," she says.

I look up at one of the postal workers, who I strongly suspect is trained to respond to emergencies but who is just standing there like he's not. My cousin was a mail carrier for years, and at his main office alone there have been stabbings and robberies and four—count them, four—women in active labor trying to get their last errand done. One was carted off in an ambulance.

"Call 911," I say, and the postal worker says, "Already done."

"Help is on the way," I say to the woman. Now other people are coming to their senses, gathering around her, putting a folded coat under her head. One guy actually goes to the counter and tries to buy stamps.

"It's too fast," the pregnant woman moans. "They won't make it." And just like that, she sort of pops. That's what it looks like. Her belly deflates, and a thing emerges that shatters and lifts and disperses weakly into the air. I say, "Holy hell," and someone else screams and this old lady behind me says, "Bees."

"What?" I glance at her package, addressed to an APO.

"That woman just shat out a whole mess of bees," she says.

I look up. We all do. The air trembles.

"A swarm," somebody says.

The bees look contained for a moment, injured or something, clumped together and hovering around a high window, maybe as stunned as we are about why they are in the post office, or how they just came out of this woman. We seem to all remember the woman at once. She's still on the floor, but now tears steam out of her eyes and into her hair. This man—one of those who was nowhere to be found when she collapsed—starts shaking her shoulders, saying, "What the hell just happened? Lady, pay attention. What happened?"

She closes her eyes.

"I'll tell you," she says.

I was having trouble getting pregnant, so I went to the healer. Western medicine, with its catheters and petri dishes, its injections and specimens, wasn't working, so I thought, Why not try something ancient? Something smarter than the present? I'd heard great things about acupuncture; friends swore by Rolfing. I found Health Keepers online—first appointment free—and drove myself because my ex and I had split up after the third year of trying. The doctor told me to call her Dipping Bird and diagnosed me with rage-based infertility. I said I didn't feel mad. She said the mind will sometimes mask the body's response to trauma, and that my body was reacting to the trauma of first being with, then being left by, my ex. A body filled with rage has no space for a baby, she said. She prescribed a wildflower honey fast, said it would promote opening and slow extraction. Rage wasn't the kind of thing you wanted to purge. The honey fast would draw it out so I could safely excrete it.

I asked how long before I could have a real meal.

She said to come back when I started to believe I didn't need to eat.

I went home with my bucket of purified honey and complimentary dipper and thought about rage. I didn't feel rage, not even in a repressed kind of way. I felt lonely. I felt tired. I felt nauseated over the big gulps of honey Dipping Bird had dosed, but that was it. My ex had been broken up over our split. I felt pity, but not rage.

Still, it worked. Like a charm, some might say. Each day I grew a little lighter. I woke up feeling happy. I put myself back together, went out dancing in the evenings. On the toilet, what emerged from my body was like tar. I could tell it was the rage. I took a little more of the honey each day, began writing poetry and smiling at strangers. I started to believe I didn't need food anymore. I went back to Health Keepers.

Dipping Bird said this was a fragile time, the intermediate period, during which I ought to be careful about the company I kept. I told her about the dancing and the poetry. She looked at me sternly. "Very careful," she said.

I wish I could say I followed her advice. I trusted her enough by then. But the thing about rage is that it can keep you alert to danger. Without it, you might let down your guard. You might, at a country line dance, lock eyes with the man wearing the biggest cowboy hat you've ever seen. The one with the sloe eyes and the obscene belt buckle. Your rage won't be there to remind you not to follow him to his car, to enjoy the weight of him on top of you until you ask to get up and can't, and he won't, and you try, and he forces, and you push, and he pushes back, and pushes, and you understand that rage is strong and sweet will not save you.

His rage will be there. Will get inside you. Will multiply in the space it finds in your body.

I was too embarrassed to tell Dipping Bird, tried doubling up on my doses instead. Thinking to flush him out. But instead—well, you see what happened. You see what is happening right now.

O

She's still on the floor. The whole post office has gone silent listening to her. Then the old woman with the APO package groans and says, "You mean for us to believe that you got pregnant with bees because you ate too much honey?"

A couple of people laugh, though it's not funny, and anyway, nobody can explain what just happened in a way that anyone's going to believe.

"I just wanted a baby," the woman says. She goes to rub her belly but it's flat now, which she is only just realizing. She sits up, perfectly fine, no blood or fluids. She searches for a pair of eyes to focus on, lands on me again. "I've had some testing done," she says, and I kind of look around, hoping she'll find someone else to receive this news. "They are not ordinary insects. They are dangerous."

"What, the bees?" the old lady says. "How come they're just sitting up there?"

"I don't know." The woman stands, dusts off her maternity jumper, which now hangs loosely off her shoulders, and resumes standing in line. She holds a stack of envelopes, and the one on top is addressed to a farm. I tap her shoulder.

"What are we supposed to do?" I say. She shrugs.

"Can't you smoke them or something? To make them less dangerous?"

"You could try that," the woman says.

The bees are getting louder, and a few people have glanced up at them and left without mailing their packages. But most of us don't want to lose our spot in line. We don't want to have to come back tomorrow. As long as the bees stay put, we're okay with them being up there.

But they don't stay put.

"Ouch," the old lady says, and we see one of the fuzzy bodies tumble off her.

It seems the bees are waking up.

The swarm unravels, a long loose thread on hemlines and letters. Before its whip can sting, I run.

When I reach my car, I sit panting in the hot box of my Honda, texting Mazie because who else would I tell?

Me: *u wont believ wht hapnd @ po*

Mazie: *TRY ME*

Me: *kiler bez came out of lady*

Mazie: *POST OFFICE ALWAYS CRAZY MONDAY*

Me: *pregnant wit bez!*

Mazie: *NEED CREAM AND BREAD*

At the grocery store I buy cloverleaf honey. I forget onions and go through the line twice. When I get home, Mazie's painting her nails. She's wearing heels and a short black dress.

"Sorry," she says, disappearing into our bedroom. When she comes out she's wearing the fluffy bathrobe I gave her on our 12th anniversary.

"Nice robe," I say, smiling.

"Thanks," she says, texting.

"Fridays are mine now."

"I know. I forgot."

I put the groceries away and start chopping onions. "Rice or quinoa?"

"I already ate."

The honey jar shines like it's lit from inside. I turn off the stove and walk out the door.

○

When I get home it's after midnight and the onions smell raw. I'm afraid Mazie won't be in bed and I'm afraid she will, so I sleep on the couch.

In the morning I wake to the sound of coffee gurgling in the pot. Mazie's sitting at the kitchen table, reading *People*'s annual Most Beautiful People issue.

"You're beautiful people," I say.

She starts to cry.

At first I'm glad. I want to say, "What did he/she/they do to my beautiful wife?" I want to remind her that this arrangement was her idea and she can stop any time. I want to ask her to wear her black dress just for me.

"Mazie, what happened?"

She closes her eyes.

It's always like this now, Mazie with her eyes closed, me watching her too closely, looking for signs. Signs that she's about to leave and signs that she's about to stay.

"Please tell me it wasn't some guy in a cowboy hat."

"I told you. I'm into women right now."

"Was her name Dipping Bird?"

"Cindi. With an *I*."

"Does she have a partner?"

"I don't know who she has."

I tell her about the scene in the post office, about the swarm of bees rising from the woman's skirt. I describe each bee in detail, giving it a name and a particular pattern. I describe them as if they weren't all alike.

Mazie's crying again. She gets up and pours two cups of coffee. Fixes mine with clouds of cream. Then she sits with her eyes closed, fingers wrapped around her cup. It's always like this now, Mazie with her eyes closed, changing. I wait for her. I stay the same.

I think maybe she's in love with Cindi.

I decide to start sleeping with that woman.

With bees.

O

Tracking her down is easy enough. I plug in a few words and news swarms my screen. Everyone's version of the story is different. It's a hoax, a prank. She's gone off her meds. She's an environmental activist calling attention to the plight of the bees. She's an alien host. She's possessed. She's a clown. She's an actress in a DIY film. She was hired by the post office to boost sluggish sales.

But I was there and I know what I saw. She gave birth to bees on that dirty tile floor.

Easy enough to find her address. She's on Facebook. She tweets. I park two blocks away. It's not stalking; we're polyamorous. Mazie sees other people and now I do, too.

Except no one answers my knock. Except as I stand on her stoop I get the feeling I'm being watched. Then I hear it: an unkempt sound. A buzzing, a slur. The window shakes. They're inside, pressed against the glass. The whole house vibrates. I call her name.

"Gina!"

"Who is it?"

"It's me!"

"It's bees?"

I hear her inside, rattling the door. I try the knob, pull with all my weight. "Push," I shout. "Give it all you got."

Years later, our daughter refuses to believe that we met mid-swarm, that she was conceived in that danger.

The bees she's seen are artificial.

"Like birds?" she asks. "Like clouds? Like sky?"

With Storm

A girl fell in love with a hurricane. Its eyes convinced her it was more than just bluster. Their color changed according to what it ate—brown for lake water, blue for sea—but in them she imagined a clear day. She thought if she could tame it, they could be a couple. A little wetter than most; a little fiercer. Harder to justify to the fam. It wasn't as if she'd chosen to fall in love like this. She'd rather someone who wasn't hell-bent on splintering her white picket fence. Someone who could stand at an altar without destroying it. But this had just happened. She couldn't explain the science of how love worked: the cogs of it, the gears. All she knew was that the hurricane did more than make her carpet wet. All she wanted was to lay naked on her roof. For glass to shatter.

She decided on capture. One day the hurricane blew in, dripping and smelling of lake water. Wearing a necklace of teeth. Iron in its hair. The girl stood outside holding ropes. Caught the thing off guard. Ringed it around the waist and pulled it gently, gently

through the door. But the hurricane didn't take well to domestica-
tion. The neighbors heard breaking dishes, screams. They saw the
bruises dotting the girl's limbs like islands. Still she wouldn't let it
out. The neighbors shook their heads when they saw her stomach
balloon. No one came to help her labor, and it was a good thing
because what the girl begat was more storms. Hundreds of them.
Thousands. They spilled out of her like marbles, dense and blind.
They swarmed, darkening day to night.

With Locust

First my neighbor's kids dropped Kool-Aid in the fish tank, turning the water blood red.

Then I found a frog in my bathtub.

Next, I got lice from trying on hats at the sporting goods store.

Then I woke up to flies on a pie I'd left cooling.

After that, an outbreak of mad cow disease at the petting zoo.

Soon I developed a feisty case of what my doctor called "adult acne."

Finally a tree fell on my car during a thunderstorm.

"Why have you forsaken me?" I cried into the phone. The automated voice at the insurance company droned on.

At work I listed my misfortunes to all who'd listen, joking about a plague of locusts.

"Well" said Daniel, "That would make sense. You've just listed the first seven plagues of Egypt."

"I'm glad I'm an atheist."

"Whatever you do or don't believe, maybe you shouldn't discount the metaphor."

After work, Daniel and I had sex for the eighth time in as many years. It was a ritual when his wife went to Aspen. But this time, even though we used a condom, I knew I was pregnant. I could feel it happening.

"Daniel, did you feel that? A special feeling?"

"Did you come, too?" He pulled on his pants.

I walked home through the garden instead of taking the bus.

I knew I was different from the beginning. It was a slow build. I didn't have any of those other symptoms, morning sickness or exhaustion. The bump in my abdomen didn't grow. Not until the seventh month, anyway.

What I did get was a buzz. The noise, which thrummed just under the skin. But also in the way people say when they get drunk. I was giddy. Lightheaded. I couldn't see well or make sense, and I loved everybody.

I loved everybody. Suddenly I couldn't get enough love. I threw myself at the bartender, the UPS deliverer, the librarian, my neighbor. I understood later that I was making a swarm.

They were everywhere, in my elbows and earlobes. Behind my eyes. The buzz in my ears came from my ears. Sometimes wings grew out with my fingernails. I was infested. Infected. There was so much exoskeleton inside my body that I crackled when I walked.

The good thing was that I had a lot of time to prepare. The bad, that I didn't know what I was preparing for. It might happen the traditional way, with me belly-up on the exam table. Or they might burst right from my skin. I'd watched the nature videos. I'd seen how they did it in the wild. But nobody knew whether or not I was the wild.

Behind my eyes, their beady black eyes. In my hair, their lacy wings.

My skin began to itch, and no amount of lotion would make it stop.

I began to understand I was going to molt.

◯

My skin began to feel like a sweater I needed to take off. I held onto the couch and pulled myself through my back. Stepped out. The shell clung to the couch arm. I was brand new. My skin was shiny and olive-colored, and I had brown hair now instead of blonde. I knew without looking that my eyes had darkened. There were other changes, too: smaller breasts, darker arm hair. An ass. I could feel my body weighted to the other side and knew that I was left-handed. The locusts were still inside, and would be for months still. I was in it for the long haul. But I was someone else now. It kept things interesting.

The bartender and librarian liked me just the same. The neighbor was loyal to the old me and kept asking where I was. I couldn't just point her to the shell still attached to the couch, so I said I was a new roommate. She was okay with that, but she wouldn't even let me put an arm around her.

The UPS delivery guy changed every time, and frankly, I didn't get that much mail. So he didn't matter.

The neighbor—a woman named Helen—kept coming over to
check on us. She wanted to make sure I was settling in. She brought
me a zucchini bread. She asked about the old me a lot. She'd been
in love and I hadn't even known it.

I had the nagging feeling that the current skin wasn't right, so
it was no surprise to me when it became clear I was going to molt
again. I noticed the symptoms from before: the locusts inside qui-
eted down so that suddenly I could hear again—I didn't realize how
much I'd become accustomed to the buzzing until it was gone—
and they stopped moving around so much, too, so that everything
felt still and eerie for several days. I didn't want to see anyone, and
when Helen came knocking, I didn't answer. She became worried,
called the house repeatedly, but I couldn't answer. I didn't want
to talk to anyone. Something big was happening inside, and it
required all my concentration.

Each time was like its own birth. The first time, it didn't hurt,
and that made me feel better about the possibility that the locusts
would be born that way, through the skin. It was satisfying, like
pulling off dead skin or a layer of dried glue. Like when I'd once
made a wax mold of my hand. Like finally shedding a scab.

But the second time, it did hurt. Not a lot. Enough to notice.
Enough to make me worried about the future.

I'd never read the Bible, but kept thinking of what Daniel had
said. At work he hadn't noticed my hair, my skin; but he'd grabbed

my ass and pushed me up against the fire door. We were fucking in a supply closet when the power went out

"C'mon," he pleaded, "lemme finish," so I did, crackling, buzzing around him, pulling him inside me harder, until he groaned; harder, until he stiffened to a shell. I pulled him through me, and even though I couldn't see a thing I knew his skin was shiny and his hair was brown.

Wings whirred between us.

He'd left his shell standing between a mop and a broom.

"You get used to the buzzing and you can eat anything."

We walked outside. The whole city was dark, blackout including stars.

"Darkness is nine," he said. "There are ten plagues altogether."

"What's number ten?"

"You don't want to know."

○

We walked all night, and if we sounded like a swarm, it wasn't on purpose.

"We can't paint every door in the city," Daniel said. "There's not enough time and not enough red."

"Didn't you say I should think metaphorically?"

"Okay. Who are the slaves and who sets them free?"

"Maybe cows? Like, cows that die and get turned into hamburgers?"

"Cows are totally slaves," he agreed. "So we should slaughter a whole bunch of sheep and smear blood on cows' foreheads."

"We're not doing that, Daniel."

"My wife's still in Aspen. I mean, no one can see us. You smell so good."

We came to the corner of a four-way stop. Even through darkness we could see that one of the stop signs was twisted backward, an accident waiting to happen. I reached up and righted it.

Electricity sizzled through our wings. Buildings blew fuses and stars smoldered. Neon rained down, hot pink and fuchsia and magenta, staining doorways and passers-by.

"One good deed," said Daniel, excited. "That's all God wanted."

I thought it was the Department of Transportation, trying to get things fixed on the cheap.

O

The next day at work Daniel acted hungover, like he didn't remember a thing.

I took a sick day and went home early.

That night Helen brought me lasagna. I waited for her to say that she loved me. Instead we helped her oldest, Moses, with his homework. Then we sat on the stoop and talked through the night.

With Fox

I was pink and you were blue.

Sometimes you were pink and I was blue; sometimes we were rain or snow together.

Our vows were simple. The sky wore white. We didn't care if it was legal to marry.

Years later, I found your ring in a field, engraved with forever, a word that means future; future a word only humans misuse. Animals live in a sensory globe. Your ring meant nothing but stone-in-the-snow.

Seven years after we'd been married for six, you admitted what we both suspected: something inside you was half something else. You were neither pink nor blue, but an orange blur chasing a rabbit through a frozen field.

You chose the needle over me.

In the thick of your thigh, in your toes like a junkie.
I lost you to fox, to fur and wander.
You turned animal before my eyes.

O

We agreed that if you turned feral; if you turned on me; if you bit and drew blood; if, then, you no longer knew me.

I promised to cage you, set you loose in a field.

We were in the kitchen; I was cooking dinner. All week you'd come home with squirrels, limbs limp. I pulled grocery store chicken from its cellophane wrapper and you raced to my feet from your nest by the door. Your stare; your pounce; your snare-trap mouth. You mauled the chicken but first you mauled me: serrated my ankle with rows of sharp teeth.

Before I set you loose; before I watched you break for the tree line; before I let you go knowing you'd vanish, I tried to tell you I was pregnant. Even though you'd bitten me and might bite again; even though you no longer recognized my voice, but saw me only as hands that opened the door to the cold place where dead things hung from hooks; still I wanted you to know. So I rubbed a towel under my arms and between my legs and spit, thinking you'd know by my scent that something inside me was also fox, and growing fast.

You tore the towel from my hands, ripped it to shreds.

That night I fed you doctored meat.

I didn't sleep, but drove for hours while you dozed in a cage. When we reached the forest, I sat in the car. You needed to be awake when I opened the door, releasing you; you needed all your senses to enter the forest. Maybe I also thought you'd say goodbye in a language halfway between our two languages.

But when I readied the cage door, you lunged; all of you already wild, and me your prey. So I tied a length of rope to the door of the cage and freed you from the safety of the suicide seat.

You vanished into the twisted trees.

I bent double, belly in fox-knots, four legs kicking at once.

Everyone expected a small furred fox; I went to that hospital, spoke to those doctors. The birth felt like a dreamscape of needles. I watched you vanish over and over, my ankle throbbing, feeling your mouth from our human days.

Even in my birthing fog the doctors seemed subdued, too quiet. I heard a cry and asked to nurse. What they lay on my chest looked far from fox. Not yours, but mine: a human child. They sexed it up in pink and sent us in an ambulance to the human hospital, as if I might stuff her back inside and deliver her again into a proper name.

I called her Reynard.

When they asked, at the second hospital, if I wanted the shots, I said yes.

I watched you emerge from the forest in our daughter. You, as you'd been before fox and fur; before puncture and snarl; before your orange goodbye. The you I'd loved first, the one you said wasn't you. And hadn't I, you'd asked me, always sort of known? I didn't tell you that the uncertainty was exactly it, why I'd fallen, the maybe this and maybe that, the way you leapt—slyly, some might say—between worlds. I'd loved the pink and the blue, the fox and the not; the things you could string onto your name; the shadow selves. How good you were with animals and children. How, in the days before you fell on all fours, you touched me with still-familiar hands as if to memorize the sensation of human touch, its careful insistency, its plurality, each finger an organism in need of gratification. To you, its growing tedium; memory, a word consigned to me; your world now all instinct, all behavior. I remember how it was your animal self that first attracted me. How perfect for me you were, because of it.

Yes, darling, I'd always known.

And seeing our daughter, I knew it again. The bridge of your nose appeared on her face. Your brow. The bow of your mouth, and there, too, your pout. Your sneer. That sideways look, the way her lip curled—slyly, some might say.

When she was small, strangers told me how handsome my little man was. I did not correct them.

When she was old enough to ask about the shots, I said they were vitamins.

Often, I went into the forest where you'd disappeared. I wasn't sure the lifespan of a fox, if you had offspring of your own, litters of this and dens full of that. Half-siblings of my one-and-only. I'd sit still for a long time, listening. You never came bounding out for reunion, of course; you never licked my cheek or nosed my hand or offered your silky head to be petted. I wasn't surprised. I'd known and not known to expect this. Known you were animal; not known how thoroughly you'd gone.

O

I always planned to tell her. But milestones became illnesses became school years became holidays, and though I felt every second with her entirely, the time to tell never came. I told myself I wasn't ready to let her go, if letting go was what she would choose. I could not bargain with her, not for cage or woods, not for wild or gone.

I intended to tell her, but not yet, not yet.

There came a time when she could've looked it up herself, the contents of her shots printed on every bottle. But she didn't.

The shots to keep her human; to keep her tongue limber, her language intact; to keep thumbs and belief; to keep her in one piece. To keep her here, to keep her mine. Sometimes I thought the word, like a bark.

Mine.

She delivered the news via email, past tense: gone off. Caffeine, runny eggs, soft cheese. And of course, those shots. As if she knew. As if the secret wasn't secret.

I waited to see what would happen to her. I didn't think to wonder what would happen to them, those babies burrowing into her body, extracting their own lifelines. Their accordion chromosomes, their genes dominating and recessing.

How many? I said when she phoned, post-ultrasound. And they're sure? They were wrong about me.

What do you mean about you? she said.

Even then, I couldn't tell her. The words in my mouth like extra teeth: bite, cage, disappear.

I said, They thought you were a boy.

I said, They sent us to the wrong place.

I could say I wasn't strong enough to do for her what I did for you. I could say she was my child, and so it was different. But the truth is that I'd already lost you twice, to fox and to feral, and I could not stand to lose you again.

I remembered the smell of the fox hospital—ammoniac, skunky. She was still in the bed, my Reynie, litter in arms. Them: already tumbling, gnawing, dragging out the contents of my purse. And yes, it's true, something about them familiar. The you that wasn't you smiled at me from our daughter's face; the you that was, nipped at my pant leg. The nurses wheeled in crates lined with bedding. I held our daughter's hand while they wheeled the crates back out, a bundle of fur now housed in each. They'd be held until after vaccines, after the controversial neutering.

How do you feel? I asked her.

She squeezed my hand, gave me a sad look. Like a mom, she said.

The hospital thought it best for her to go back on the shots immediately.

She wept. Consented. I told her, We will bring them home. We will fill the house with chew toys, feed them chickens and grapes.

She said, What can I possibly teach them about the world?

I touched her hair, like yours but thicker. There are things we can do. To make them more teachable.

I don't know, she said, and I said, You are their mother. You know.

But she didn't.

So we ended up in the woods together, ropes in our hands, the suicide seat.

Afterwards, we drank tea, shivering. I said it was better this way, though I knew she didn't want my comfort, moral a human method for giving meaning to nothing, no meaning here to be had. I presented her with a syringe of it, the stuff we could use to wipe away the human grief.

She shook her head. That's not us, she said, but it pained her to say it. She turned from me, and I watched the woods open up around us. I saw her start to leave me in the most human of ways.

With Plush

The twins sleep with animals. The girl wants a lion at the foot of her bed and the boy wants a bear stuffed down his PJs.

I'm pregnant, he says.

My lion ate a tiger for lunch, she says.

We choose a story together, one of their favorites, about the world before us, the world that built now. Dinosaurs and furry people. Carriages, typewriters, men without wombs.

I shut the door quietly and go into the living room. My wife is knitting a computer on the couch. I grow some potatoes in the insta-farm. After dinner we punish the robot for talking sass.

I miss sweetness, I say.

Do you miss witch burnings, too?

Our husband chimes in. *You two. Always bickering.*

I change the subject, something I've been practicing in compassion class. *Time for bed. Let's pick our plush.*

My wife wants a gazelle. My husband wants a zebra. I want a sloth, so we go into the zoo room and unlock the cages.

Then we hologram nostalgia porn: a man talks on a phone that's attached to a wall.

With Sloth

So much sleep; your eyes slid shut. I wanted to lick you, but you were always sleeping. I wanted to fuck the way we did before baby, before the thing in your belly took over our nights.

Still it was adorable how your hair grew thick and you tied it back with garbage bag twisties. Still it was adorable how you unleashed your cravings: pumpkin and pretzels; seaweed and dirt.

You were 55, too old for a human child. Your choices were lemur, ferret, or sloth. Weeks of research and you opted for sloth. You were planning on *S* names: *Steffi* or *Sid*.

The sloth inside you grew by stealing your sleep. It wanted to be born so it could sleep even better. You swore you felt its silky fur. *Like a pillow*, you said, as you snoozed the alarm.

Sometimes at the mall we'd see parents with humans who looked just like them. Tiny versions of Mommy or Daddy, crying and shoplifting. Throwing tantrums in line. You were *S* for *sad* when we passed Baby Trinkets. *Look at the cute*, you said. *Miniature socks.*

I converted the guest room into a nursery: hammocks, perches, baskets, soft beds. Soon our child would hang from a ladder while the other hand shoveled food in its mouth.

Sometimes people touched your belly without asking. When we passed a human parent with an animal baby you fixated. Once you cooed at a woman tossing sticks for her dog.

What a lovely baby.

My dog's not a baby; she's a shelter rescue. You animal mothers are the worst kind of breeders.

That night at home you cried, asked me if she was right; were you selfish, wanting one of your own?

Love's not selfish, I said, rubbing your shoulders. Wanted to ask: *How come I'm not enough?*

For the first time, you took a public stand on an issue, answering phones for Pro-Animal Life. You joined the pet sitting debate: *Can pet sitters babysit animal babies?* You boycotted the Boy Scouts (animal babies=no) and praised the Girl Scouts (animal babies=yes). You chanted *We're here, we're parents, get used to it!* You put stick figures on the station wagon: you, me, and an animal blob.

Nights, we watched videos of a sloth sanctuary in Costa Rica: sloth yawns, pleading eyes, sluggish bites of green beans.

Sunday afternoon was animal parent support group. Tuesday night was birthing class, which made us both nervous. We were the only couple expecting an animal child.

I hate having to educate people when I'm just trying to live my life.

Yeah, but who better to educate people than us?

You smiled, the smile that seduced me 29 years ago, when we met at a wedding. You were the bride; I was not the groom. After your honeymoon, a hasty divorce. I'd never been part of a scandal before, but it suited you, with your scarves and tight skirts. You were an artist, and everything you painted came alive on canvas. Now that your imagination had a blood supply and your art was part of your body, I was merely the frame, wood and wire that held everything together. Who notices a frame when seduced by a painting? The frame should disappear; and I did, over the kitchen sink, washing dishes while you slept; scrubbing the tub while you tried out *S* names. You moved through the world with an attention to animals that made humans recede. Sometimes *humans* meant *me*.

My friends joked that if I was a furry, I'd get more attention. But your focus wasn't sexual, it was maternal. And your maternal instincts seemed to cancel out sex with me, the human you'd loved for nearly three decades. I missed being everything to you. I resented our child, your child, your sloth, little *Sally* or *Samuel*. In dreams I woke up to find myself caged, while the house filled with sloths: at my desk, in our bed.

I decided to sit down and try to tell you my feelings. First I bought a tacky card, something of a joke between us. On the cover were two stuffed bears (sloths apparently weren't popular on greeting cards), with sad faces and broken hearts and sparkles that came off on my hands when I opened the cover. Inside: *I Miss You. Let's Be Beary Close!*

You loved things like this. *K* for *kitsch*. I put the card on the kitchen counter. I took a walk around the block, stopped in at the grocery.

When I got back, you still weren't home from your studio. An hour, two hours. Sometimes you stayed late, but you always texted. By nine o'clock I set off toward the waterfront. You worked in a warehouse filled with art studios, upstairs from a lumber supply company, a bike shop, and a tiny bar.

The lights were on in your studio; I was relieved. Then I noticed blinking from the alley out back. An ambulance and a crowd around it. I shoved my way past bikers and wood.

It was a dumb idea anyway, you said a few days later, when, home from the hospital, you sat on the couch. You were in your fluffy robe, my blue plush slippers falling off your feet. I made pot after pot of peppermint tea.

We could adopt, I said, then added, *a baby.*

I don't need anyone but you, you smiled.

We curled up together. It was like old times, but it wasn't, really. Now I knew. I knew that I hadn't been enough all along, that something was missing, and would always be missing. *S* for *stolen.* I would leave someday, because you couldn't, because you didn't know how.

Anything's possible, you said.

Or I could choose to believe you, to live in invention. The way we pretended that you were pregnant with sloths. The way we'd invented a world full of animal babies.

We sat watching people walk by our window, children and dogs and hipsters and thieves.

With Raccoon

I was 143 feet in the air when I felt the blade. The first swipe missed, but the second drew blood. Someone was squatting in the cab of my crane, aiming to stab me as I climbed up the ladder. A few summers ago ecoterrorists burned down rows of condos in Fremont and Wallingford. If they set fire to my crane I'd be burned alive.

My foot slipped on a rung and I swung from my harness until my feet found metal. Glancing up I saw two giant raccoons peering out of the cab. They'd made a nest in my L&I sweatshirt. I wondered if worker's comp covered rabies shots.

My supervisor glared when my feet touched dirt.

Early lunch? You just clocked in.

Tell that to the raccoons hanging out in my cab.

After that, forget getting anything done. Someone called wildlife rescue; someone else called the news. Reporters showed up, hustling for footage. Our union rep sent everyone home.

O

When I got to the apartment, my wife was cleaning the kitchen. She looked pretty, gray hair falling out of a clip. Her mouth had that determined set.

Chrissy's learning to tell time. Little hand first.

I kissed her forehead. *Time's important.*

O

People live in rooms I've lifted. Walk on beams I've flown through air. Every day I climb 150 feet above concrete and steel, all the lights of my city. Alone in my crane I'm pregnant with buildings. But sometimes the view seems to beckon me down. When Chrissy died, I thought about jumping. My depression was gravity; I knew it could kill me. Raising buildings was part of staying alive. If I could bring buildings up to meet me, there'd be no jumping and nowhere to fall.

My wife just disappeared inside. She'd quit her job to homeschool our daughter. When Chrissy got cancer they lived together, just the two of them, in an apartment close to the best hospital in Seattle. After Chrissy died, Cora kept the apartment, everything just as Chrissy left it. She spoke to our daughter, read her stories at bedtime. Every morning she sat at the table and taught lessons to an empty chair.

So I sold our house, moved in with Cora and our daughter's ghost. Into a building I'd built with my crane. The doctors said I needed to be gentle but firm. They suggested pills to numb and distort. But I loved Cora, and we loved Chrissy, and who am I to say what's real?

Take the raccoons, for instance. The day after I spotted them they were gone. I climbed up the ladder, two crew members behind me. We carried cages and we carried bait. The raccoons left nothing but the nest they'd made out of my sweatshirt and my chair's torn cushion. I wondered if they dreamed of jumping, if the view was seductive, if they wished they could fly. The crew member behind me said, *Goddamn vermin. You see them things? Big as dogs.*

Yeah, I said. *I saw them.*

They were gone, but all day I felt them. Like that tingling in your spine you get when you're being watched. I'd seen raccoons waddling through the crosswalk at night, trailing babies, daring oncoming traffic not to stop. Some pests you got the feeling were too dumb to be scared, but not raccoons. *Go ahead and try*, they said, fat lolling. *You can't get rid of us.*

The inside of my crane smelled like their piss, their love. They were watching me, waiting. For their babies to be born. For me to tip backward on the ladder. *Do it*, they said. *It don't take nothing but letting go.*

Chrissy's acting out today, Cora told me. *She got three X's on her chart.*

She pointed at the refrigerator. There was a behavior chart under a couple magnets. It hadn't been there yesterday. The magnets were all of animal rear ends. They'd been a gift for Chrissy.

She's going to need a talking to, my wife said.

I kissed her forehead. *I'll take care of it.*

I was in the news footage. I had a sneer and sunken eyes. Hat head. I pounded on the crane. *They almost took me out*, I'd said, but the news cut that part. Left just the image of me, pounding my machine. The drizzle made my shirt look stained. Everything about it was wrong. I looked exactly like I was supposed to.

It was the thing that bothered me most these days: being the parent of dead girl meant I was not a parent at all. Other moms and dads put on the patient voice they used for childless people when they talked to me about their kids. If I said, My daughter used to do that, they'd smile and ask how old she was now. So I didn't talk about her. I figured I got enough talking about her at home with Cora anyway.

But it weighed me down, those conversations. Made climbing the ladder to my crane difficult. Made looking at that picture of me on the news, pounding my crane like an animal, especially hard. I didn't know who that guy was. I didn't know why it mattered.

If I ever saw those raccoons again, I would bring them down.

Cora hadn't left the apartment in years. *Honey?* I said when I got home. *Sweetheart?* No answer.

She returned a few hours later, her coat unzipped. Hair windblown. *Chrissy took off. I chased her all the way across town.*

I kissed her forehead. *It's good to get out.*

She looked up at me. I mean right in my eyes. *I saw you on TV.*

Oh yeah? The raccoon thing?

Watch out, she said. *I hear most of them have rabies.*

I think these ones are okay.

That's what they think, too.

O

I got her point. What did raccoons know of illness? They move their nests away from danger and let that be enough.

O

Except they came back. The next morning, climbing the ladder, I noticed a flutter of movement above. The kind of thing where when you look, it's gone. But I knew enough to brace myself, and when I got to the top, I edged inside real quietly. Didn't breathe a word of it to the crew below. I thought maybe it would be nice to have company up there, like a pet or something. But these weren't pets. They hissed at me, lunged again with those razor claws. Then they took off out the window. It took me a full ten minutes to realize they'd left the babies on the floor next to me. They still had their eyes shut.

The parents hadn't gone far, and were now watching me from a hemlock across the way. I went about my business lifting beams, swinging them past the raccoon couple and into place. The raccoon babies shivered and mewed like kittens.

Three of them. I was so mad at the parents for leaving that I wanted to throw the babies over the edge.

Learn how to watch your kids, I yelled to the parents. *And stay out of my damn cab.*

By the end of the day, they were gone. The parents had retreated into the branches. I hated them. I knew how tough vigilance was. I'd wished for relief. I'd wished for relief in whatever shape it took, and later beat myself up for thinking that way. But you didn't just give up.

Then I noticed that the babies were gone, too. I ransacked the cab, but there was no trace of them. I even looked over the edge for evidence of my own carelessness. A sharp turn that'd flung them out? An unconscious kick? They were just gone, and I got the feeling I sometimes got after Chrissy died, this disturbing sense of having made the whole thing up.

Cora didn't return until the middle of the night this time.

I lost her, she said.

What do you mean? I said. *Chrissy's gone?*

She kissed my forehead. *Don't worry. I'll find her again.*

You hear stories of kids crawling up cranes. Getting stuck like kittens. It seems impossible, but the news stories don't lie. They show us exactly what is possible.

When they called me about Cora, I didn't believe them at first.

She refuses to come down, they said. *She said she's looking for someone.*

They had the squads, the news, the fire trucks. I thought that was it, she was going to jump. I was almost jealous. It was hell to lose a kid. She had an out, a real one, and it proved to me that mine had been fake all along.

I climbed the ladder to Cora. I told the EMTs to wait on the ground. *Give me fifteen minutes with her*, I said. *If I can't get her down, you can do it.* They listened to me. She was my wife.

There were things I thought might happen when I got to the cab. Like that we might symbolically throw Chrissy out the window. Or that we would decide to divorce. Big things; irrevocable things. I thought we might join hands and jump together. I thought I might tell Cora she needed more help than I could give her.

But when I got up there, she smiled at me like she used to when I came home from work, and for a moment it sent my heart soaring. I climbed over her, and she took my hand, and we sat there, like we were waiting for the fireworks to begin. We sat for a long time, not talking, pregnant with these things that plagued us: raccoons and buildings and grief. Maybe pregnant is the wrong word. We were infested with them. Infected.

After fifteen minutes, the EMTs climbed back up.

Cora and I sat tight. There was nowhere else in the world we needed to be.

With Hippo

It was my job to open the box when someone pushed the red button. An alarm went off, and I rushed to the nursery. The buzzer went off at least once a day, garbage, pranks, and false alarms. Three babies abandoned in the past nine months, but most of the time I found headless dolls. Pink flamingos, plastic swans. Once a stone lion fuzzy with moss.

I couldn't see inside the box from the nursery, so there was also that creepy blind moment of reach. I took a deep breath when I opened the door.

Some countries called them baby hatches; in medieval times they were foundling wheels. We called it The Box. We called it The Button. We called them The Clients. And babies were Saved. Not saved in the religious sense, although some of my co-workers talked about Jesus. But they weren't the ones who opened the door to find condoms and gum stuck to the heat lamp. I didn't think we were angels of mercy. Mistakes with heartbeats are just hard to undo.

When I wasn't opening the box, rehoming stolen statuary, or bottle-feeding abandoned babies, I was a teller. Like a fortuneteller, but with cash, not cards. Unfortunately most peoples' fortunes were small. I worked at a bank because I worked at a bank. There were other jobs, but they seemed like celebrities. I imagined doctors and sailors at parties, white coats so bright they had everyone fooled. At least I had health insurance and a 401K. If I was bored at work, that just made me humane.

The box was outside, by the ATM. Anyone could open the door, set down a baby, and press the red button. Once they shut the door, it locked. Warm blankets and heat lamps kept the temperature toasty. The inside door opened onto the nursery, which we created out of a supply closet.

When we voted to install the baby box, everyone's life got a little more interesting. It stopped us from worrying about People With Guns; it stopped us from joining the Occupy movement. We had a new cause, which made management happy. They'd soothed us without adding dental or vision. It was better than Facebook or smoking on break. When the alarm went off, whoever wasn't working would follow me into the nursery and wait while I twisted the key. Sometimes they wanted to stick their hands in, and bring out the baby. I made them wear gloves, powdery latex, pulled over their wrists with a snap and a sting. Always junk; no one else rescued babies. Only me, and only alone.

Also, the three times I'd rescued living, breathing human infants, the alarm hadn't gone off.

"Coincidence, huh?" Marisol was the office manager. She was grumpy before 1 o'clock.

"Makes sense to me," Lewis said, texting. "The parents didn't want anyone to see them, so they just ran off."

"Whatever. I'm on to you, Sadie." Marisol clicked her tongue to her teeth.

The three living, breathing human infants had all been wearing clothes from Baby Wear World. They'd all been clean, and surprisingly cheerful. Everyone cooed over them; and me, for my amazing rescue. Then people who wanted a baby drew straws. Kaylee got the first one, a girl she named Kayla. Then Robert took home little Gwendolyn Lou. The third baby went to Michael, who named him Ernie, middle name Bert.

It was great to see Kayla, Gwen, and Ernie so happy, especially when they'd come from such terrible situations. Sometimes, when another baby went missing from the mall, we'd post the newspaper clipping in the break room next to pictures of Kayla, Gwen, and Ernie. So sad! So sad that someone was stealing babies from shopping carts in Baby Wear World!

I just couldn't help it. Who leaves their kid in a shopping cart while they run down to the other end of the mall for a cheese pretzel?

It was a test. When someone agreed to leave their baby with me while they went to the Food Court, I knew that baby belonged with a better family, with parents like Kaylee, Robert, and Mike. I took them from the cart because they needed to be found. I put them in the box so someone would find them. That someone was me, which made it all perfect. I planned my trips to the mall weeks in advance.

One Tuesday I was daydreaming behind bulletproof glass, debating whether a weekend was too risky, when the alarm went off and didn't stop. Usually it beeped five times, then quit. At first I thought it was a car alarm, but the noise in the nursery was almost unbearable.

I was alone in the nursery when I opened the box.

At first I thought pug. Then potbellied pig. Whatever it was, a miniature something, it was gray-black and breathing, too big for the box.

I reached for it, scared it might bite, but it was stunned, too scared to turn on me. I set it down in the crib and stroked its hide. *Hera. Hera the Hippo. Hello.*

I went to the employee kitchen for the formula we kept in a cabinet with the plastic forks and napkins and spare birthday candles. By the time I'd warmed up a bottle in the microwave, the alarm started going off again, so I rushed back to the nursery and opened the box. This time, a note.

We hope you enjoy your new baby hippo! Hippos need water so their skin doesn't dry out! Your new hippo will drink warm milk, but DON'T heat it in the microwave, as this can cause heat pockets that will burn baby!! Hippos need a lot of love but watch out—they can become aggressive!

Then, in small print at the bottom: *Hippo is to be kept on premises at all times. Hippo may not interact with customers. Your emergency exotic animal veterinarian can be reached at the number below.*

I crumpled the note. I didn't care if it was some ploy from management. Hera was here, and she was mine. There would be no drawing straws this time, no goodbyes to choke back. I went to the crib, where Hera was gnawing on a bumper. She did look a little dry. I shook the bottle to break up any heat pockets and tested the temperature on my arm. I left the bottle wedged between the crib slats and went back to the front desk. Emptied the candy dish and filled it with water.

Hera put her feet in the dish and tipped it over, soaking the mattress pad.

She needs a tub, I thought.

"She needs a tub," I said.

The alarm clanged. I opened the box.

Kiddie pools work great! the note said.

On Monday, Marisol avoided me so conspicuously that I knew she'd been the one to turn me in. She seemed surprised to find me in the kiddie pool, but not to see the hippo. She patted its rump and splashed her fingers across the water for Hera to follow.

"It's like a mascot," Kaylee said from the door. "If banks had mascots."

"She," I said.

"What?" Kaylee said.

I stood up, pulling my bathing suit down in back. "She's a she," I said. "Not an it."

Michael walked in, and Kaylee gave him a look. His phone buzzed in his hand and he glanced at it instead of her. "Ernie just smiled," he said. "Do you know that hippos defecate in the water?"

Marisol removed her hand from the pool. I picked up Hera and held her. Her skin felt like candle wax. "So does Ernie," I said.

Kaylee tried to give Michael another look, but he just nodded. "I hate when he does that."

"Kayla said dada," Kaylee said, taking a step closer to me. "She's only five months."

I set Hera on the floor, and she walked up on my feet and stayed there, making little grunting sounds when she breathed.

"Hera and I have begun to form a bond," I said. "Eventually, she'll attack anyone who comes near me."

Marisol, Kaylee, and Michael walked out. I prepared to warm Hera's next bottle.

Two things became clear: they weren't going to fire me, and I didn't have to work. I stayed in the nursery taking care of Hera all day, then went home to watch *Law & Order* reruns. I slept in and returned midmorning to give Hera her breakfast. A couple weeks of this, and the alarm went off again. The box provided a rubber-banded bunch of hay and some kind of kibble that I put in a bowl on the floor—*Two cups a day!* I realized I hadn't heard the alarm in days. I'd been distracted; Hera was growing fast. Now pictures of her covered Kayla, Gwen, and Ernie and their respective newspaper clippings. Hera in a Baby Wear World dress. Hera on her back in the crib with her legs in the air. Hera wearing sunglasses. Hera carrying a baby doll in her mouth. I'd taken all the pictures, so there was only one with me in it. I'd fallen asleep on the floor feeding her, and she'd climbed on my back. My face was in my arms, so you couldn't tell it was me, but I was the only one she'd climb on. We all knew that.

Sometimes I forgot I was in a bank, and I'd go up front to tell Michael something cute Hera had done—the time she got hay stuck to her forehead, the time I let her lick a lemon and she made a face—and get stares. Maybe an older lady at the counter covered her mouth like I smelled bad (Hera had her own odor). Maybe a little kid pointed. One day I forgot myself entirely and walked Hera right up to the lobby. She was about the size of a cocker spaniel by then, and she ran up to this pregnant lady in line and just *rammed* her. I didn't know if it was because the woman was pregnant, or because she was wearing red, or what, but Hera plowed into her so hard that she knocked the woman over. Hera snorted and bellowed and bit the woman's arm so hard she drew blood. She wouldn't quit until I carted her off.

The note that came through the box that evening was harsher than usual: *Under no circumstances is Hippo to interact with the customers!!!*

I wrote back: *She has a name, and her name is Hera.*

I added, *And my name is Sadie.*

And last, *And my lawyer's name is Valerie Frank*, just in case they had anything funny in mind.

They wrote back promptly. *Whoa, we don't want any trouble here! Hippo-raising is a Fun Employee Diversion, but we are happy to send you up front again if you'd prefer! We can assure you that we're on the up and up with the law and whatnot, as all necessary permits and licenses have been filed, and building codes have been strictly enforced! No worries, friend!*

But then the food stopped coming.

The dry towels stopped coming.

The one-use cameras stopped coming.

The box sat empty, day after day, while Hera gnawed on the lip of her plastic pool.

They weren't going to fire me, exactly, but they'd quietly stopped paying me too. So when I went home to find my belongings on the lawn, I packed them into my car and drove them to the bank. Set up a table lamp and pullout in the nursery. Marisol glared; Michael helped. He showed me a video on his phone of Ernie crawling across the room. "I owe it to you for finding him," he said. He gave me an awkward, one-armed hug.

"It was nothing," I said.

"Not nothing," he said.

We grabbed the couch and lifted from our knees.

Hera liked the new furniture. She was a surprisingly good climber for a hippo. I was beginning to forget she was a hippo, in fact, since she acted more like a two-year-old. There was no money for hay or milk, so I brought her handfuls of grass from the lawn outside, but it was too green, too free of weeds, and I worried about feeding her pesticides. Hera took to standing in her pool with her face in the water. Just standing there, faking submersion. Maybe practicing holding her breath. Quirky, like a two-year-old.

When she got sick, finally, I called the emergency exotic animal vet. The line rang and rang. I didn't want to tell the others, so I gave her some baby Tylenol and hoped for the best. She got worse. She nibbled at the grass in her bowl, then threw up; nibbled, threw up. Stood in her pool with her head under water. Then lay down. I pulled her onto my lap, which she was too big for now. She'd sprouted a fine layer of hair, so that now she was candle wax and feathers. I loved her like a two-year-old. As much as you can love something you can't really understand.

"You'll be okay," I said. "Because you have to."

She snorted. Looked at me as if to say, *You* have to.

But of course, I didn't really know what she would've said. She wouldn't have said anything. She was a hippo.

It was their fault, the note-writers, for making her sick. For taking away her vet. But still, I felt like a bad mother.

I didn't mention any of this to my co-workers.

They say a child's death is the worst thing. They don't say anything about a hippo's death. But for me, Hera's death was the worst thing.

She lay in the water. She didn't get back up.

I walked out of the bank. I had no money.

I went to the mall. Baby Wear World was full of people who stared at me. I smelled like a zoo. I looked like I hadn't showered in a long time because I hadn't. I understood without asking that no one would leave their babies with me today.

I asked the clerk for an employment application. He gave me a funny look and said they weren't hiring.

So I followed a group of women pushing strollers, followed them right out of the store. Fat baby arms beat rattles on their trays. Sockless feet kicked. I trailed them to the food court, where they bought pretzels and parked their babies at the next table, facing out. I watched the babies, and then I watched the women not watching their babies, and then I made my move.

With Nebula

You are there and not there. Visible on one ultrasound, nearly gone by the next. On the movie screen over the examination table, a haze of lights, constellations flashing and whirring, everything so busy, pulsing and sliding and shapeshifting, bone and muscle, brain and tissue. And off to the side, next to all the motion, I see you: a pebble of solidity. A seed. A mass of motionlessness, dark.

You are Baby B. A vanishing twin, in the process of unbecoming. I can watch it on the screen, the fade, the shrink, the way you are beginning to condense and condense into what never was. Bits of you flaking off. You could be anything at all: goldfish, planaria, star. A mixed-up mash-up of genes, animal and human, human and astral, real and un-. Whatever it was, it didn't work. The word the ultrasound tech uses is *reabsorbed*, though the more I think about it the less sense that makes. You are not being absorbed again—the first time was a striking out, a leap, the opposite of assimilation. You will not go back the way you came. You move into new territory, fanning out. Part of me and not part of me at all, the way the healthy one, the human one—Baby A—becomes. There she is, though I don't yet know she's a she, thrusting forward, broadening, differentiating. Separating into detail. The line between us so clear, so easy to locate on this map.

Not so, for you. You'll have no labor, no birth. Instead of pushing, we relax. Instead of contracting, we expand. Each cell becomes less distinct but more itself: you will never be anything but Baby B. This dense knot. These broken strands of DNA unwinding, these peeling layers—face and sex and potential—released into the wilds of my body. My body, where there is only and always the two of us, which is one of us, which is you vanishing and me, gravid. You are the part of me that recedes over and over. I can stay here as long as I like, the ultrasound tech says, and I think I would like to stay here, perpetually full of you, unable to hold and yet always holding you. Without touch, like breath. Like fullness. You are buoyancy and flux. You are the opposite of weight.

With Animal

In this version she's not a virgin, so the immaculate conception is harder to explain. The difference is that she's only ever been with women, and though she's participated in plenty of original sin, it hasn't ever, to her knowledge, involved sperm. But there are all those lingering doubts. Easier to believe that she'd been had, tricked into coitus without knowing it, than that the baby came from God. Never mind that she'd woken one day covered in tattoos, vines winding around her arms, clematis and hibiscus and passion flower. Never mind that she suddenly smells death everywhere. She's not even a religious person. She's as skeptical as the next person of people who don't realize they're pregnant until the baby is born.

She doesn't realize she's pregnant until the baby is born.

She knows something is wrong, but she thinks it's illness and is afraid to seek help.

She feels swollen and weepy, but blames it on the old chicken she ate from the fridge.

She craves tree bark and clover, but takes a Vitamin C supplement instead.

Sometimes she wets the bed. She blames that on lack of sleep.

But when she finds herself driving into the country because a dream angel told her to, then she knows this is beyond explanation. She pulls over to collect herself in a motel parking lot. It's the middle of the day but there's no one at the front desk, so while she waits she crosses the street to a place called Joe's Petting Zoo. There are camels, the sign says. And sheep. A man at the barn takes her dollar and asks when she's due. "What do you mean?" she says, and like that, she gets a sudden urge to push.

In this version, the manger stays the same.

She gets on all fours to deliver. There's nothing peaceful about it, just slop and goop and grunting. This time it happens in broad daylight. She is totally naked, feeling as though her whole body is ripping in half, the camels placidly observing. She doesn't know what's happening, and after it happens, she's still not sure. This time what emerges is a bundle of fur and claw that immediately scurries further into the back of the barn and hides. She can't even see it. She's exhausted, the pressure of the afterbirth on its way, the dogs at the door growling. The man crosses himself with her dollar. When the placenta drops with a splat, her first reaction is to taste it. But the man is watching, so she doesn't.

The camels are bigger than she'd thought camels would be. She crawls between their legs, looking. *Baby*, she calls weakly. *Come here.*

No one in this version sings hallelujah. No one says unto you. But it's true that when she finds the animal it is surrounded by light. There is no name for what she sees but she knows, at least, that the name is not human. It's huddled in hay in a corner of the trough. Something tells her to pick it up. Something tells her to carry it out of the barn. Her baby is large, heavy. Outside, daytime stars shoot out of nowhere. She is alone and dripping. The man is on his phone—maybe 911, maybe animal control—so she knows she has to get the hell out of there.

In this version her child has feral teeth and prickly paws that grope for teats.

In this version she prays to the florescent lights of the motel lobby. Steals a towel and the key to room 12. Shakes the vending machine for pineapple juice and fish-shaped crackers. Her room has a view of the waterless pool.

She swaddles tail and snout in the stolen towel. Her baby doesn't cry, just curls and uncurls its paws, kneading air. She isn't sure how to feed it. With breast, with blood? Should she prick her thumbs? This isn't happening. She'll never love it. Holds it, breath against her chest, fur warm as sun. Her baby mews, gropes for her pulse. She feels something shatter inside her, ice shaking loose. She's drowning in it, all the water in the sea inside. Drowning in how much she loves this child.

She uncovers its face, big pig-sloth-dog.

She's in love and names it *Unexpected*.

Requited. Tornado. Jesus. Online.

She paces the room, trying on names. Finally she settles on Mary Todd Lincoln. In the bathroom she notices the sink is filled with warm water and a bottle of milk. Taped to the bottle is a note: *With Child.*

Mary Todd takes to the bottle like a pro. Slurps contentedly, spitting bubbles. Burps. Falls asleep on the flowered bedspread, pillows around her for a makeshift crib.

The sound of the vacuum in the hall gets louder. There's a knock on the door. She wraps herself in a sheet and peers through the peephole. Light floods her eye and she turns away.

Housekeeping. Would you like more milk?

Yes, thank you. She opens the door. There's a cart filled with bottles, soft blankets, clean clothes. *Bless you,* she says, but the hall's deserted. She drags the cart inside and bolts the door.

While Mary Todd sleeps, she explores the room. The mini fridge is stuffed with wafers and wine. There's an enormous suitcase in the corner with a note: *In Case Of Emergency.* She peels back the curtains. The pool is gone (was it ever there?), replaced by a gas station and the glare of the freeway. There's a Gideon Bible on the nightstand, next to an old-fashioned phone with a rotary dial. For kicks she dials "o," as if Operator.

How may I direct your call?

Thanks for the milk! What time is check out?

The o hangs up.

The TV doesn't work.

○

In this version she's all three wise men, dressed in a pink sweater, orange t-shirt, and baggy jeans. In this version she wears neon green sneakers with pom-pom socks.

Now Mary Todd is sitting up. She's a cross between a pit bull and a baby panda.

○

The cart arrives each morning, but no matter how quickly she opens the door, the hallway's empty. She rushes inside, bolts the lock, counts the bottles. One day there's a glass jar of baby food; then soup, simmering in a shiny pot.

So this is what it means to be a saint, she thinks. She blows on the soup. Mary Todd latches onto the spoon and gnaws.

○

Now she's teaching Mary Todd to read. They speak animal twin speak, mewls and soft moans. Together they turn the fragile pages of the leather-covered Bible. Sometimes Mary Todd gets rough, rips a page, and eats it. Sometimes they stand by the open window, each time a new view: mountains, skyscrapers, sprawl.

She can't decide if she's one of the missing: girl on a milk carton, six o'clock news. Sometimes she dreams of her last, best ex. She misses sex. She misses her dog.

○

She decides to escape. After all, nothing's really keeping her here. Sure, the motel seems to be traveling through time and space, but that's probably an illusion. She wants a better life for her daughter. She wants Mary Todd to go to school. She wants playgrounds and play dates, a garden, a swing. She may be holy, but this isn't heaven.

The suitcase, she thinks. She stands over it, staring. Touches it gently like a feverish child. Six thick locks click open at once. She lifts the lid, sees a mass of brown hair.

A wig. And a child's dress, pink with lace trim.

The phone rings.

Hello?

Check out, says o.

She opens the door. The hallway is crowded with travelers, with room service and housekeeping and someone refilling the vending machine. This is what parenting is, she thinks: you stuff your animal into human clothes. You walk into the world disguised.

What a beautiful girl you have. So pink.

Mary Todd smiles, showing animal teeth.

Acknowledgments/Notes

Carol:

Thanks to Lisa Ahmari, Bruce Beasley, Bellingham Bikram, Oliver de la Paz, Alison and Bruce Fitton, Mary Ann Graflund, Suzanne Paola, Debra Salazar, Nichola Torbett, Ann Tweedy, and S.L. Yannone.

Special thanks to Gerry Guess, who took my writing seriously from the very beginning.

Special thanks to Heather Franklin for love and inspiration.

Special thanks to Kelly Magee for co-parenting this collaboration.

Special thanks to Elizabeth J. Colen for everything.

Kelly:
Thanks to Maria Ridley, Joy Langone, Tim Magee, Cassie Quest, Erin Magee, Lauren Kenney, and Kami Westhoff for their support, encouragement, and love.

In memory of Marjorie "Chick" Berry, friend to children and animals.

Thanks to Carol Guess for being a fabulous co-writer.

Carol and Kelly:
Thanks to Britt Ashley, the Critical Animal Studies Work Group at the University of Washington, Justin Daugherty, Marc Geisler, Bruce Goebel, Sara Greenslit, Tiana Kahakauwila, Ben Loory, and the Creative Writing faculty and students at Western Washington University.

Thanks to the Nonhuman Rights Project:
www.nonhumanrights.org

Special thanks to Todd Horton for allowing us to use his artwork on the cover: www.toddjhorton.com

Special thanks to our publisher Diane Goettel; our book designer Amy Freels; and all at Black Lawrence Press for their faith in this project.

Thanks to the publications where these stories first appeared:

"With Animal," *Hayden's Ferry Review*
"With Cat," *Word Riot*
"With Dragon," *SmokeLong Quarterly*
"With Egg," *Bloom*
"With Fish," *Passages North*
"With Fox," *Indiana Review*
"With Hippo," *Storm Cellar*
"With Horse," *The Adirondack Review*
"With Human," *Juked*
"With Jellyfish," *Sundog Lit*
"With Killer Bees," *Gravel*
"With Locust," *Spittoon*
"With Me," *Communion*
"With Raccoon," *Animal Literary Magazine*
"With Replica," *3Elements Review*
"With Sheep," *Among Animals: The Lives of Animals and Humans in Contemporary Short Fiction* (Ashland Creek Press)
"With Sloth," *Heavy Feather Review*
"With Snakes," *Front Porch Journal*
"With Sparrow," *New South*
"With Spider," *Jersey Devil Press*
"With Squirrel," *Arcadia*
"With Stone Lion," *Zero Ducats*

Photo: Heather Franklin

Photo: Lauren Kenney

Carol Guess is the author of fourteen books of poetry and prose, including *Tinderbox Lawn*, *Darling Endangered*, and *Doll Studies: Forensics*. In 2014 she was awarded the Philolexian Award for Distinguished Literary Achievement. A frequent collaborator, her co-authored collections include *How to Feel Confident with Your Special Talents* (with Daniela Olszewska) and *X Marks the Dress* (with Kristina Marie Darling). She teaches in the MFA program at Western Washington University, and blogs here: www.carolguess. blogspot.com

Kelly Magee is the author of *Body Language*, winner of the Katherine Anne Porter Prize for Short Fiction, as well as the collaborative poetry collections *The Reckless Remainder* and *History of My Locked Wrist*. She teaches in the undergraduate and MFA programs at Western Washington University.